THE
MANILA
DECEPTION

A James Acton Thriller

D1699937

Also by J. Robert Kennedy

James Acton Thrillers

The Protocol
Brass Monkey
Broken Dove
The Templar's Relic
Flags of Sin
The Arab Fall
The Circle of Eight
The Venice Code
Pompeii's Ghosts

Amazon Burning
The Riddle
Blood Relics
Sins of the Titanic
Saint Peter's Soldiers
The Thirteenth Legion
Raging Sun
Wages of Sin

Wrath of the Gods
The Templar's Revenge
The Nazi's Engineer
Atlantis Lost
The Cylon Curse
The Viking Deception
Keepers of the Lost Ark
The Tomb of Genghis Khan
The Manila Deception

Special Agent Dylan Kane Thrillers

Rogue Operator
Containment Failure
Cold Warriors

Death to America
Black Widow
The Agenda

Retribution
State Sanctioned

Templar Detective Thrillers

The Templar Detective
The Parisian Adulteress

The Sergeant's Secret
The Unholy Exorcist

The Code Breaker

Kriminalinspektor Wolfgang Vogel Mysteries

The Colonel's Wife

Delta Force Unleashed Thrillers

Payback
Infidels

The Lazarus Moment
Kill Chain

Forgotten

Detective Shakespeare Mysteries

Depraved Difference
Tick Tock
The Redeemer

Zander Varga, Vampire Detective

The Turned

THE MANILA DECEPTION

A James Acton Thriller

J. ROBERT KENNEDY

For the over half-million civilians and military personnel who died in the Philippines during the Japanese occupation in World War II.

THE
MANILA
DECEPTION

A James Acton Thriller

"People of the Philippines: I have returned. By the grace of Almighty God our forces stand again on Philippine soil—soil consecrated in the blood of our two peoples. We have come dedicated and committed to the task of destroying every vestige of enemy control over your daily lives, and of restoring upon a foundation of indestructible strength, the liberties of your people."

General Douglas MacArthur upon landing in Leyte, The Philippines
October 20th, 1944

"I pray for the Emperor's long life and prosperity forever."

The last words of Japanese General Tomoyuki Yamashita
February 23, 1946

PREFACE

During World War II, the Imperial Japanese Army systematically looted the conquered territories in Southeast Asia. This included government and bank holdings, museums and galleries, as well as private holdings. The scale of the theft was massive, totaling by some estimates in the hundreds of billions of dollars.

This substantial hoard was consolidated in Singapore, with plans to move it back to Japan to finance the war effort. When the war turned against the Japanese, plans changed, and the stolen valuables were believed to have been transferred to the Philippines where one of the men largely responsible for their looting had been transferred to stop MacArthur.

General Tomoyuki Yamashita.

There is no disputing the hoard exists, as the looting is documented. There is also no disputing that the vast majority was never returned after the war, meaning it is either still out there, or has been found and that fact hidden.

There is one claim that the treasure had been found in the Philippines by a man named Rogelio Roxas, then stolen by President Ferdinand Marcos. This led to a court case filed in Hawaii that led to, at the time, the largest judgment in history, amounting to $40.5 billion with interest. The Appeals Court summarized the original judgment with these words:

"The Yamashita Treasure was found by Roxas and stolen from Roxas by Marcos' men."

Yet even that alleged discovery couldn't account for all that was stolen.

Leaving an unanswered question.

Where is the rest of Yamashita's Gold?

Mindanao, The Philippines
Present Day

"Everybody down!"

Archaeology Professor James Acton extended his arms and herded everyone toward the rockface, the large stones from an earlier collapse providing some cover. He was desperate for a weapon, yet if any of them were armed, they would likely be killed.

Their only hope of survival was to stay out of the line of fire.

Shouts erupted from their private security, their Tagalog a language he didn't understand, yet they sounded professional and calm.

Something he certainly didn't feel, his heart slamming, his ears pounding. He draped himself over his wife Laura, Tommy doing the same with his girlfriend Mai, and a surge of pride in the young man rushed through him.

He too was willing to take a bullet for the woman he loved.

Gunfire erupted from the jungle and he spun his head to see what was going on. The three members that remained of their security detail returned fire as they took cover, though judging from the muzzle flashes from the thick trees and the night sky, they were vastly outnumbered.

Somebody cried out and one of the defensive positions fell dark. Mai was sobbing now, Tommy was shaking, and the man that had brought them here, the man that had assured them they'd be safe, was curled up in a ball on the ground, muttering to himself.

And their chief of security was headed away from their camp and to safety.

Another cry, then only one gun remained, and it fell silent moments later. The steady fire from the jungle stopped and the sound of their attackers advancing echoed through the now silent jungle, even the creatures that filled it quiet.

"Everybody just stay calm. No threatening moves. You know what they said. We'll be taken hostage if we just remain calm."

Acton stood, raising his hands, then turned to face their new captors.

"We surrender."

14th Area Army—Shobu Group Headquarters

Baguio, The Philippines

October 25, 1944

"Well?"

Sweat trickled down Captain Takuma Kijima's back, even more than usual, the heat and humidity today oppressive to say the least. Normally temperate at this time of year, Baguio City was experiencing a heatwave, and they were all paying for it. He had grown up near the foothills of Mount Fuji, the son of a distinguished local official, allowing him the luxury of a university education. And that had meant a commission when the war broke out.

Though none of that had prepared him for the heat of the Philippines.

And now his commanding officer, the man he served as his aide, was expecting good news.

And he had none to give.

"I'm afraid we lost them all."

General Tomoyuki Yamashita paled slightly, his mouth agape at the unexpected news. "All?"

"Yes, sir. An American submarine intercepted the convoy and all the cargo ships were sunk."

General Yamashita's shoulders sagged as he dropped into his chair, gripping the arms. "How much did we lose overall?"

"Almost twenty percent."

Yamashita shook his head. "We can't risk the rest. We need it to finance the counterattack."

"Will there be a counterattack?" Kijima immediately regretted the question as Yamashita bristled, his knuckles turning white as his fingernails dug into the arms of his chair.

"You doubt the Imperial Army's ability to defeat the Americans?"

Kijima snapped to attention, his shoulders thrust back, his chin high. "Never, General!"

Yamashita sighed. "Then you are alone in this room."

Kijima's eyes widened, though he remained at attention.

And silent.

Yamashita gestured toward the door. "Close the door then sit. We must come up with a plan."

Kijima closed the door, but remained standing, instead walking over to a large map of the Philippines tacked to the wall, the latest troop positions indicated, including the Americans who had just landed in Leyte, led by that devil MacArthur.

They were losing the war, though no one wanted to publicly admit it lest they be executed. Yet the general himself had just suggested he too had his doubts.

It was shocking.

Yamashita had defeated the British in Malay and Singapore in only 70 days, earning the nickname The Tiger of Malaya. During his tenure there, he and others had organized the systematic looting of the newly conquered territories of Southeast Asia, amassing an incredible fortune and collecting it in Singapore for transport back to the homeland.

Yet everything had changed when supremacy on the seas had been lost to the Americans. When Yamashita had been reassigned to the Philippines to halt the American advance, a series of daring missions were undertaken to sail the treasure to his new command, with the intention of leapfrogging it back home through Taiwan or China.

It was a plan that had run out of time.

The Americans commanded the sea and the air, and the test run they had just attempted had failed miserably, an American submarine taking out the ships with ease.

There was no way they were getting the gold off these islands.

And there was no way they could leave it for the Americans to find once the Imperial Army was inevitably defeated. The vast amount of gold and riches would finance the American war effort, and could lead to the ultimate defeat of Japan itself.

He shuddered at the thought.

"What are you thinking?"

Kijima turned to his commander. "We must hide it."

The general joined him in front of the map. "Agreed. But where?"

Kijima pointed to the port in the south where the gold was currently held. "The confiscated items are here, in Cotabato, on Mindanao. Two ships are still loaded, ready for the next run should the first have proven successful. Rather than unload them, I suggest we move them here." He pointed at the nearest port to their current location, San Fernando. "That way, in the highly unlikely event we do retreat, we can take it with us, and the gods willing, we will succeed in at least bringing a portion home with us."

Yamashita frowned. "And the rest?"

"The bulk is still offloaded, stored in a warehouse." He pointed at the map, deep in the interior of Mindanao. "There are a lot of caves in the mountains. I saw them when I was first assigned here."

Yamashita leaned closer to the map. "It seems remote. Difficult terrain to transport that much property."

"Yes, but that's the advantage of it." He moved his finger slightly. "There is a small village here, perhaps a couple of hundred people. Other than that, there's nobody in the area to see our ultimate destination. Anyone else along the route would simply assume we're another convoy, moving troops or supplies. No one would ever know we were storing the gold in the caves."

Yamashita tapped the map. "Except the villagers."

"We could…eliminate them."

The general regarded him for a moment. "You are an unforgiving soul, Captain."

Kijima bowed crisply. "I serve the Emperor."

"And you do it without question." Yamashita shook his head. "No, a massacre leaves too many questions unanswered, including the all-important one."

"Which is?"

"Why."

Kijima sighed. "You are correct, of course, sir. What would you recommend?"

"A massacred village will force people to ask why we killed them? What were we trying to hide? An *empty* village forces people to ask where did they go? Why did they go? It forces people to look elsewhere, as opposed to where they already are."

"Forgive me, General, but I don't understand."

Yamashita pressed his finger on the map, the knuckle turning white. "You put them here."

Kijima's eyes narrowed for a moment then flared, his mouth agape as he finally understood. "I will execute your orders personally."

The Lotus

Yakuza Owned Establishment

Tokyo, Japan

Present Day, Three days before the surrender

Takashi trembled with fear. There was no other way to describe it, for he was more terrified at this very moment than he had ever been. When he had initially borrowed the money—something he now would freely admit was the stupidest decision of his life—he had been scared. The implications of borrowing money from the Yakuza, what Westerners might describe as the Japanese mafia, were severe. Not paying them back was an option one didn't dare contemplate, and at the time, he hadn't.

For he had been certain he would succeed, and pay the loan off with time to spare, despite the onerous interest.

"You're late again."

Takashi nodded, feeling faint, his skin clammy and cold as he battled his bladder's desire to free itself of its contents. "Y-yes, I know, and I'm sorry, but—"

"But what? You made a commitment, and you've failed to live up to it. 'But' suggests you have an excuse. I'm not interested in excuses. I want my money."

"But—"

"Again with the buts." Akira, the eldest son of the Yakuza *oyabun* for the district, shook his head, looking around the room at his entourage, all standing around the walls, all packing. "I'm a nice guy, right?"

A round of confirmations circled the room.

"I'm a patient man, right?"

More confirmations.

Akira stared at Takashi. "Have I not been patient with you? Have I not been a nice guy with you?"

"Y-you've been both, sir. It's just that when we made our agreement, I didn't realize you would also be demanding—"

"Demanding?"

Takashi paled. "I-I mean, requiring—"

"Requiring? Remember, I'm a nice guy. A patient guy."

"Y-yes, of course. Umm, requesting…?"

"I like that."

"Requesting protection money also be paid. When I opened my restaurant, I never thought I'd be not only paying back the loan, but paying protection money as well."

Akira shook his head. "But we're offering you a service. Have you been bothered by anyone else? By the police? By the health inspectors? By local thugs?"

"N-no, and I appreciate that, but—"

Akira tossed his head back, his blazer opening, revealing a shoulder holster filled with as large a pistol as Takashi had ever seen. "Oh, how I hate that word!"

"I'm s-sorry, but—I mean, not but, umm. I don't know what to say!" Sweat trickled down his back. "I thought taking a loan from you to open my restaurant meant automatic protection."

"It did. We provide protection to secure our investment. However, protection is never free. You do understand that I'm running a business here, not a charity."

Takashi's shoulders slumped. There was no point in arguing. And it wasn't safe to do so. He remained silent.

"You have until the end of the week to pay back the loan in full."

Takashi's eyes shot wide. "End of the week!"

"You are in arrears. You know the terms."

His pulse raced as his stomach churned. "I-I have no way of paying you back. Not that quickly."

"That is unfortunate. Defaulting does happen, though I would have thought you had learned from others who have done so that it isn't wise." Akira sighed, glancing at his men. "I guess another example is necessary to remind others what young Takashi here has forgotten."

Heads nodded.

Akira pointed at the door. "End of the week, or face the consequences."

Takashi stumbled from the room, blind to the world around him as his pulse pounded and he lost focus. He was going to die. The amount of money was simply too much.

He needed help.

Yet from whom? His parents didn't have money like this, even if they sold their home—something that couldn't be done by the end of the week, regardless. His grandparents were both dead, and he had no siblings.

And no rich friends.

There was no one he could go to for money, nor confide in for advice.

Hiijiisan!

His eyes widened slightly as he pushed his way through the dancefloor, thick with revelers, the Yakuza bar always doing a brisk business at this hour. His great-grandfather, his *hiijiisan*, was nearly 100 years old, yet he had a sharp mind, and generations of experience.

He might know what to do.

And he was at least a safe ear to speak to.

Mindanao, The Philippines
November 5th, 1944

Captain Kijima ordered the driver to stop in what could tenuously be called the center of the village. If the village had a name, he wasn't aware of it. His map merely had a reference number, and any future maps produced wouldn't even have that.

He stepped out of the truck and pulled at his shirt, the sweat causing it to stick to his body. He could never get used to the heat. Yes, a summer back home could get hot, but nothing like this.

It was the humidity.

Part of him wished the war would end soon so that he could return home to his wife and son, yet that could only happen if they lost.

A year ago, if anyone had asked, he would have thought them crazy for even suggesting the possibility. And promptly ordered them interrogated then executed. But today, with the Americans making rapid inroads, and intelligence rumors of further landings, their days were numbered, despite the hundreds of thousands of brave Japanese soldiers willing to lay down their lives in defense of their homeland.

For if the Philippines fell, then so would Japan.

It was only a matter of time.

Though *that*, he had serious doubts about.

Yes, they might lose the war, but there was no way the Americans would be willing to pay the price in blood to take Japan itself. Millions would die, for every single Japanese citizen would fight them tooth and nail before surrendering.

No, America would drive the Imperial forces back to Japan, then sue for peace to save their sons from the carnage that awaited them.

Japan would survive, though might be licking its wounds for decades before emerging once again.

Enough time for his son to become a man, and serve the Emperor in any future glory the Empire might seek.

He gave the order, and dozens of blindfolded soldiers emerged from the back of several transport trucks at the lead of the large convoy that stretched far out of sight, only the drivers witness to where they had driven, and none privy as to why. This mission was beyond top secret, though the fact the treasure had arrived in Mindanao was one he feared wasn't well kept. This was why he had diverted the two ships still laden with gold and other valuables in their holds north, hugging the coastline to avoid the American Navy, to rejoin General Yamashita's forces.

A secret intentionally leaked by the local intelligence office, with one small falsehood embedded among the truth.

That it was the *entire* treasure.

It was only another fifth, the same as had been sunk earlier by the Americans.

His large convoy held almost 60% of the treasure, excluding the artwork left behind to be destroyed if the Americans neared. Paintings and sculptures couldn't be easily liquidated to fight a war, but precious metals and gems could be. The only people who knew of the existence of this convoy were in the trucks he now commanded. Nobody at the port knew, or at least should know, though those that did had no idea of their destination.

He alone was privy to that.

It had meant a long, tiring trip on roads that could barely be called that, through dense vegetation that at times had to be cut back with machetes to proceed.

It was nearly noon, the sun high in the sky, the villagers working their rice paddies taking notice. Shouts of concern were relayed among the fields, and fortunately, for him, the villagers began to gather inside the village as he ordered his men to calmly take up positions around the town.

"Be friendly. Smile. We don't want anyone running."

A young girl ran up to him, a flower in her hand. She held it out, and he knelt in front of her, taking the gift and making a show of smelling it. He smiled and patted her shoulder. "Thank you."

She ran back to her mother who picked her up, eying the new arrivals with suspicion.

As he took in the gathered crowd, so many women and children among them, he sighed.

Not enough workers.

He turned and stared up at the hills nearby where the caves they sought were located. He had been here a couple of years ago on a survey mission, searching for caves and other natural locations that could be used for defensive purposes. Caves like those he had found here were now used to store supplies throughout the archipelago of over 7000 islands, with the intent that this would be the final stand of the Imperial Army. Here they would either defeat or delay the Americans, long enough that the defenses of the homeland would be prepared to the point America would realize the price of invasion was simply too high.

He turned to the translator he had brought with him. "Florencio, find out if everyone is here."

"Yes, sir."

The Filipino, a translator at the Japanese Embassy before the war, and who had worked for them since their arrival in exchange for food and shelter for his family, approached the locals, words exchanged briefly before returning. "Everyone is here, sir. They want to know why you are here."

"Tell them we have a job for them to do, and they will be rewarded handsomely for it."

Florencio informed the gathered villagers, now numbering at least two hundred, and smiles were exchanged.

Kijima pointed to the hills. "Tell them we need to transport the contents of these trucks to the caves up there. Everyone will be fed, and will be paid in gold when finished."

Florencio's eyes flared for a moment at the mention of gold, his greed quickly masked. "Gold, sir?"

"Yes, gold. Enough for them to feed their families for years."

Florencio smiled. "Might I help as well? To share in this gold?"

Kijima regarded the man for a moment with a mix of disgust and pity. "Why not?"

St. Paul, Maryland

Present Day

"I think this is the first time I've ever given you a lift."

Archaeology Professor James Acton grunted, again applying his imaginary brake as young Tommy Granger came to yet another abrupt halt as a result of his tailgating. He was regretting accepting the young man's offer of picking him up after dropping his car off at the garage. "And it might be the last."

Tommy didn't pick up on the commentary. "Anything serious?"

Acton shook his head. "No, just routine maintenance."

Tommy grinned. "Could be worse."

"How?"

"Professor Palmer could have forced you to buy one of those British sportscars."

Acton chuckled. "Nah, I've never been a two-car kind of guy."

"Two-car?"

"Yeah, one for me, one for the mechanic who'd have to drive behind me everywhere."

Tommy laughed then made another turn without his signal light.

Acton had had enough. "Is there a reason you don't use your signal light?"

"Huh?"

"We've been driving for ten minutes, and I haven't seen you use it once."

Tommy shrugged. "It's not the law, is it?"

"Actually, it is. And even if it isn't, why wouldn't you want the other drivers to know what you're doing?"

Tommy made another turn, the signal light clicking this time. "I don't know."

"There must be some logic."

He shrugged again. "Well, just back there I was in the turning lane, so everyone should know I'm turning left."

"Riiight, because no one ever changes their mind."

"What do you mean?"

"You've never seen some idiot decide to turn left then change their mind and go straight? You can never be sure what the driver is intending unless they have their signal light on. And if the vast majority of us use signal lights, we assume someone isn't making a turn if they don't have theirs on, so we make decisions based on that. If you then do something different, that's how accidents happen."

Tommy chewed his cheek. "Yeah, I suppose. I guess I should use it sometimes."

"Why only sometimes? Do you only brush your teeth when you're seeing people, or do you do it every day?"

"Umm, every day?"

"Why?"

"I dunno. Habit?"

"Exactly. If you signal every single time, then you get in the habit, and you never forget. That way the rest of us don't have to try and read your mind to figure out what you might be doing on the road you share with innocent people including children."

Tommy signaled again. "Okay, sir, you've made your point. Always signal."

"Good boy."

"You should be a driving instructor."

"Ugh, don't get me started about why that's a colossally bad idea. You couldn't pay me enough to do that."

"Why?"

"No patience."

Tommy glanced at him. "I always thought you were remarkably patient."

"I usually am, but trying to teach someone to drive? There's just something about it I find so frustrating."

"Who did you ever teach to drive?"

"A buddy in high school. Never again."

"Was it really that bad?"

Acton unnecessarily pointed at his driveway, Tommy quite familiar with where he was. "That's a story for another time." Tommy pulled into the driveway and Acton climbed out. "Want to come in and say hi? Laura will make my life miserable if she thought I didn't ask."

Tommy shrugged. "Sure."

They entered Acton's humble home, one he had owned for years before he met his wife, Archaeology Professor Laura Palmer, and smiled at the sight of her rushing from the kitchen and into the hallway.

"It's about time! I've been going nuts waiting for you." She gave Tommy a quick peck on the cheek. "Good to see you, Tommy."

"What, no sugar for me?"

She gave Acton a look then planted one on him that had his knees shaking within moments. "Happy?"

"Tommy, go home."

"Nonsense. You're not getting any." She shook a manila envelope that had gone unnoticed in her hand. "I think we found it."

Acton eyed her. "Found what? The lost Templar Treasure?"

Her eyes narrowed. "I thought we already found that in the south of France?"

"That was just one room of it. There was enough to fill a whack of ships."

Her eyebrows shot up. "Ooh, we should go looking!"

He rolled his eyes. "Yeah, because the fact no one has ever thought of that is why it's never been found."

She grinned. "Haha." She shook the envelope again. "And speaking of lost treasure, you remember Professor Bautista's request?"

"Buwan? About Yamashita's Gold?"

"Exactly."

Acton's heart skipped a beat as he finally focused on the envelope. "You don't mean—"

"We found something." She spun on her heel and returned to the kitchen. Acton and Tommy followed and found her poring over dozens of photographs laid out on the kitchen island, the envelope evidently an empty prop.

Acton leaned over the satellite photos with various different filters applied. "What am I looking at?"

"Satellite photos of the Philippines. Mindanao to be precise." She pointed at one of the photos. "What does that look like to you?"

"Camera defect?"

Tommy leaned in. "Godzilla's final resting place?"

They both stared at him.

He raised his hands in defense. "Hey, Hollywood wouldn't lie, would they?"

Laura sighed. "You two aren't very helpful."

Acton grinned. "We had ice cream. We're giddy."

Laura tapped his chest and he looked down at the mint green ice cream still staining it. "I'm buying you a bib to keep in the car."

"Wouldn't have helped. We were in Tommy's."

"It's a wonder I can take you anywhere."

"I yam what I yam."

"I don't know what that means."

It was Acton's turn to roll his eyes at his British wife. "We'll make an American out of you yet."

"God help me." She tapped her finger on the photo. "Do you want to know what *I* think it is?"

"Please."

"It's the site of what was once a village. A *farming* village." She moved her finger slightly. "See, this? It looks like abandoned rice paddies, and this looks like a long-abandoned village." She shifted her finger again. "And here's a river that leads to the ocean, just south of Parang."

Acton's eyes widened as he stared at the mouth of the river and the coastal town in question. "There are two major rivers coming out here, and two minor."

"Exactly. Don't you think this matches all the clues he gave us?"

"Mountains?"

She tapped her finger just north of the abandoned village.

His heart drummed with excitement. "Holy shit! Do you think you've found it?"

Tommy cleared his throat. "Umm, found what?"

Acton turned to him. "Yamashita's Gold!"

"Yam a shit a what?"

"Yamashita's Gold. A massive hoard of gold and other valuables stolen by the Japanese during World War Two, last seen in the Philippines."

"How much gold are we talking about?"

"Billions. And I mean *billions*."

Tommy grinned. "When do we leave?"

24

Mindanao, The Philippines
November 6th, 1944

Juan's parents were excited. In fact, all the adults appeared excited. Since the Japanese had arrived, they had all been breaking their backs hauling heavy crates of supplies from the trucks in the village to the caves he had played in despite his mother's admonishments. And as each truck was emptied, another from what appeared to be an unending supply arrived to take its place.

Everyone was exhausted, yet everyone persevered. He had never seen gold before that he could recall, though he must have seen a ring or some jewelry at some point and hadn't realized what it was. In his ten years on this earth, he couldn't fathom how much gold it would take to feed a family for years, though he imagined it was a lot. He had to think of it in terms he could relate to. He knew what the rice harvest looked like, how many baskets the mango trees filled. It was huge when looked at all at once.

And food was the most precious commodity he knew. Gold to him was merely a word. It was supposed to be valued, but if it couldn't be eaten, then it was of little use unless it could buy food. And food could buy food already. His family would trade rice and mangoes for other foodstuffs they required. Money never exchanged hands. In fact, he had never seen money before. Everything was barter. A bushel of rice could buy you so much at the markets of the surrounding villages and towns. But gold? What could that possibly be worth? After all, it couldn't be used for anything beyond jewelry, so why would anyone think it was valuable?

It made no sense to him, but even his family were struggling to carry the cases up the treacherous hill and into the caves while he and the other children made certain everyone was provided plenty of water as they broke their backs serving the Japanese.

He had heard of them, and a group had passed through their village when he was younger, but other than that, they hadn't affected his life until now. His parents were afraid of them—everyone appeared to be, yet other than the fact they looked different, they seemed normal enough.

Their uniforms are nice.

He handed his father a scoop of water from the bucket he was hauling. "Can I be a soldier one day?"

His father drank, his Adam's apple bobbing greedily. "To rid ourselves of these vermin, you may have to be."

"Are they bad?"

His father glanced around nervously, his eyes settling on the Filipino who had arrived with the troops. "Enough talk. Attend to your duties."

"Yes, Father."

He pressed up the hill to the next group of four carrying another heavy crate, the footpath to the caves narrow and riddled with roots and other treacheries threatening to twist ankles and break bones. The caves weren't much farther, and scores of trucks had already been unloaded, their cargos safely deep inside.

He handed a scoop of water to the first man as he kept pace, looking forward to when the soldiers left and he and his friends could examine what was inside the crates. He imagined all manner of wonders, from foods he had never even heard of, to the strange devices and weapons the Japanese carried on their person.

I want one of their swords.

A smile spread as he refilled the scoop for the next man. One of the crates had to hold swords.

He frowned as a thought occurred to him. Certainly the Japanese wouldn't want them opening the crates. After all, whatever was in them must be valuable, at least to the Japanese. There was no way they would leave these supplies here, unguarded. He took a sip of the water, his own thirst demanding attention before he shifted to the opposite side of the path to quench the other two men. It was disappointing. He had been excited about discovering the contents of what they were moving, but now he realized that he'd never be given the chance. The Japanese weren't leaving, at least not all of them.

They couldn't.

He spotted the Filipino he had heard called Florencio ahead, leaning against a tree, his contributions to the efforts lasting a single trip up the path. He decided he better offer him water lest he become displeased. Obviously, these Japanese were bad if his father thought he might have to become a soldier one day to fight them, so making any of them mad might not be a good thing.

And bypassing the man while carrying water might do just that.

"Water?"

The man nodded and took the ladle, holding it up to his mouth and drinking. He returned it to Juan. "Thanks."

"Do you like working with the Japanese?"

Florencio shrugged. "It beats the alternative."

Juan's eyes narrowed. "What does that mean?"

"It means you're too young to understand."

Juan's stomach churned with the insult. "When we're done, will you be leaving?"

"Yes."

"All of you?"

"Yes." Florencio shoved him back toward the column of villagers hauling the supplies. "Get back to work."

Juan scrambled back up the line, catching up to his position, but not before he had a sudden realization.

They were all leaving.

All.

That meant no one to guard the crates.

A smile spread.

It meant he would have some exciting adventures after all.

His father glanced at him as Juan pushed up the line to regain his position. "What are you smiling about?"

"That man said they were all leaving when we're done."

"So?"

"So, that means we can see what's inside the crates when they leave."

His father stared at him for a moment, then his eyes widened with a fear Juan had never before seen.

"What's wrong?"

His father quickly shook his head. "N-nothing. Move along. There are thirsty men ahead."

Juan complied, rushing up the hill, left to wonder what had his father so scared.

St. Paul, Maryland

Present Day

"Can you send me the images?"

The excitement in Professor Buwan Bautista's voice was obvious to them all. Professor James Acton laughed with glee at his wife and Tommy Granger, all huddled around the phone set to speaker. "Not on your life!"

Disappointment replaced the excitement. "Why?"

"Because then you wouldn't need me to bring them to you!"

Bautista roared with laughter, a burst of static momentarily overwhelming the speaker. "Jim, if you and your wife want to join me, you are more than welcome. But I must warn you, we're on a shoestring budget here. Nobody here believes the gold exists, so it would just be the three of us."

Acton chuckled. "Well, I don't know if I believe you either, at least not until a few minutes ago. Everything you told us about, we found, or more accurately, my wife found."

Professor Laura Palmer leaned closer. "Actually, it was a colleague at the Smithsonian. And as to funding, if you would permit us, we would be happy to make a donation and bring equipment."

"No no no, I can't ask that of you."

"Please, it would be our pleasure. We have some money set aside for just these things."

"If you insist, then who am I to say no when I'm so desperate? When can you be here?"

Acton replied. "Tomorrow. We'll arrange the jet then send you the details."

"Arrange the jet? Don't tell me you have a private jet now!"

Acton laughed. "Things have changed quite a bit since we last met, my friend."

"Well, I know you're still a lowly archaeology professor, Jim, so I'm guessing you married well."

He winked at Laura. "You have no idea." She squeezed his knee. "Listen, I'll text you the flight details as soon as we have them."

"Wonderful. I'll start preparing everything at my end. I look forward to seeing you again and meeting your lovely wife. Until tomorrow!"

"Goodbye, my friend." Acton ended the call and leaned back in the stool at the breakfast bar. "I'll start putting together an equipment list, you make the flight arrangements."

"Can we come?"

Acton and Laura both stopped what they were doing and turned to Tommy. "Excuse me?"

"I'd like to come, and I'm sure Mai would too."

Acton frowned at the mention of Mai Trinh, Tommy's significant other, and a young woman he and Laura had taken under their wing when she had been exiled to America after helping them escape her native Vietnam several years ago. She was like the daughter they couldn't have. "I'm not sure if that's such a good idea."

"I agree," said Laura. "This is Mindanao. It's not exactly the safest of places."

Tommy shrugged. "Safer than Mongolia."

Laura wagged a finger. "Safer than Mongolia turned out to be, yes, but Mongolia isn't inherently dangerous. Mindanao is different. Things could go south in a myriad of ways."

Tommy folded his arms. "Well, if you're so concerned about the possible dangers, then I assume you're going to bring some security with you."

Laura looked at Acton. "We probably should."

Acton had to agree. The Philippines wasn't exactly the safest of countries, and where they would be traveling, there were Islamic groups active in the area. "I think you're right. Do you think Cameron can get there in time?"

"I don't know, but I'm sure he can join us before we head to Mindanao. We should spend at least one night in Manila to acclimate."

"Then it's settled," smiled Tommy. "We should be safe with him, shouldn't we?"

Acton sighed, regarding the young man he had grown quite fond of. He was a graduate student at his university, and was the love of Mai's life. If these satellite photos did indeed point to Yamashita's lost gold, it was a once in a lifetime opportunity for all of them. He turned to Laura. "If we find it, it's history-making."

She was forced to agree. "It is."

"Maybe the kids should come."

Laura shook her head. "Well, you're both grown adults, I guess." Air burst through her lips, causing them to vibrate. "I just wish we weren't so rich."

Acton's eyes narrowed. "Why?"

"Because then I could use the excuse that we couldn't afford their tickets."

Mindanao, The Philippines
November 6th, 1944

Chatter was rippling up and down the line, and it was clear to Juan that any excitement once held by his elders was gone, though he wasn't sure why. Any time he would approach with water, they would fall silent, then resume as he left.

It was frustrating.

He hated it when adults protected him from the truth. What was so dangerous about it? His mother always told him to tell the truth, and if he were caught lying, his father would give him the back of his hand.

So, why protect children from the truth?

He spotted his mother ahead, the women coordinating things at the bottom and top of the hills, making sure everyone was fed, and providing extra water or repairs to footwear, along with much-needed shoulder massages.

He paused. She was scared too, her eyes darting between the Japanese soldiers gathered around the cave entrance, and the men of the village as each group arrived with yet another crate, disappearing into the gaping maw of the cave.

It suddenly took on a different aura, that of a beast swallowing the adults, and it took him a few moments to realize why.

No one was coming out.

Earlier in the day, there had been a steady stream of eager men entering the cave with their heavy loads, then reemerging with smiles before grabbing a quick snack and some water, then heading down the trail to fetch another load.

But no longer.

Now even he was concerned.

He glanced back and spotted his father cresting the rise, his body drenched in sweat, the fear from earlier still pasted on his face. His father glanced at him as he passed.

"Go to your mother, and be ready."

"For what?"

"Do what she says."

"Yes, Father." He followed him toward the cave entrance. "Father?"

"Yes?"

"Why aren't the men coming out of the cave anymore?"

His father stared ahead for a moment, then cursed. "Go to your mother, now!" he hissed, and Juan complied, his little legs carrying him across the rock-strewn clearing and toward the gathered women.

"Where are they?" asked his mother as she held out a hand for him. "Nobody has come out for at least fifteen minutes."

"I have a bad feeling about this," said his aunt.

"What are we going to do?"

"What can we do?"

She placed a hand on his back, holding him tight against her, and he freed himself of the water, hugging her as hard as he could, his entire body trembling as he realized something truly was wrong, and that the adults were all scared, including his mother and father.

Maybe protecting me from the truth is *better.*

His father passed them, and his mother pressed him even harder against her.

"Get out of here," whispered his father. "They're going to kill us all."

Nails dug into his back, but he suppressed the whimper as his father's words sent jolts of terror through his body. The women around him all began to mutter, the panic growing, a panic not lost on the Japanese soldiers surrounding the area.

The last box, carried by four men he had grown up with his entire life, crested the hill and slowly followed his father through the cave entrance, one last look exchanged between him and his family before the darkness swallowed him whole.

His mother grabbed his hand. "Stay quiet, and do exactly what I say."

"Yes, Mother."

She slowly stepped backward, toward the trees that lined the clearing. He followed, his breath held as his heart hammered, when she yanked his arm, sending them sprinting into the jungle. He struggled to keep up, his mother saying nothing as branches and leaves swatted at him, the undergrowth thick.

Shouts erupted behind them, then loud cracks rang out, the trunk of a tree to his left exploding as it was hit by something. He had heard gunshots in the past, though they were nothing like this.

He slowed.

"Hurry!" cried his mother, yanking him forward once again. They were following them now, the sound of men crashing through the forest overwhelming in his panicked state.

He was slowing her down.

They would be caught because of him.

"Hurry!"

He pressed forward, trying to keep up, but his little legs were simply too short. She stopped and gathered him in her arms then continued their flight, yet it was no use. From his new vantage point, staring over her shoulder, he could see the soldiers closing the gap. More gunshots sounded in the distance, though it wasn't from their pursuers.

"They're going to catch us!"

Tears filled his eyes with the terror he now felt, yet he wasn't certain what he should fear. It was clear his mother didn't want to be caught, that his father thought these were bad people, but what did it mean to be caught? Did it mean death? And what did that even mean? Wouldn't that simply mean they'd all be together again in Heaven?

A shot rang out and his mother stumbled, falling to the ground, trying to cushion his fall. She pushed to her knees then pointed forward. "Go! And no matter what you hear, don't come back!"

"But I want—"

"Go!" she cried, the soldiers now only feet away. He turned and sprinted into the thick jungle as his mother screamed, the men upon her. The pursuit stopped as he heard more screams then laughter.

Laughter?

He stopped, hiding behind a tree, and stared back. His mother continued to scream, and he was old enough to recognize the difference between agony and terror.

And he heard both.

Yet the men continued to shout and laugh.

It made no sense.

He slowly walked toward the noise, creeping forward from tree to tree, whatever horrors his mother was going through growing louder as the laughter continued, and though he couldn't understand the language, he recognized the tone of men encouraging other men onward.

His jaw dropped as every muscle in his body slackened at the sight ahead. His mother lay on the ground with one of the soldiers on top of her. He recognized what was going on, even if he didn't understand it.

His mother was being hurt. He continued forward, urine streaming unnoticed down his leg, when his mother twisted her head to rid herself of the soldier pressing his mouth against hers.

And their eyes met.

And he screamed.

Tokyo, Japan
Present Day

Takashi's great-grandfather's heart ached for him, the story spilling out between sobs and gasps for air terrifying. He remained silent in his chair, his oxygen tank by his side, the tubes pushing the vital gas into his nostrils long forgotten.

Yet the story had his failing heart pounding too hard.

He grabbed the mask sitting on his chest and pushed it against his mouth, taking a bigger hit of the oxygen, feeling its effects immediately.

"What can I do? I just don't know what to do! I think they're going to kill me."

He nodded. "They will kill you, my boy, they will kill you. The Yakuza of today are not those of when I was your age. There was integrity then. They never would have tricked you like that. It is dishonorable. A disgrace." He wagged a boney finger. "But you were a fool to go to them. To get yourself mixed up with the likes of them, you should know better!" He coughed, Takashi leaping to his feet to help, but he waved him off, instead sticking a tube in his mouth and drawing some water. "Have you spoken to your parents?"

"I'm too ashamed to."

"You must. This man you owe money to might decide to come after them for your debts."

"Even after he kills me?"

"Yes. They should know so they might take steps to protect themselves."

"What about me? What steps can I take?"

"You must go to the police. Tell them everything."

"They'll kill me for sure! Even if Akira is arrested, his men will still get me. He's the oyabun's eldest son! Surely they'll kill me!"

"I see little choice."

Takashi shook his head. "No, I can't go to them. If they kill me, they might spare my parents. And can we trust the police? Don't the Yakuza have people on the inside?" He threw his hands up in the air. "If only I had something of value! Something I could give them! But even if I sold my restaurant, it wouldn't be enough. The interest alone is more than it's worth."

He exhaled slowly, his eyes closing as his foolish descendant's words triggered a thought. He did know something, something of value. Something of great value. Something that might satisfy the Yakuza.

If they believed it.

"I may have an idea."

Takashi leaned forward eagerly. "What?"

"It is my greatest secret." His chest tightened as his eyes burned. "And it is my, Captain Takuma Kijima's, greatest shame."

Mindanao, The Philippines
November 6th, 1944

Captain Kijima supervised the herding of the remaining women and children into the cave, when several of his men emerged from the jungle dragging a half-naked woman and a young boy. He frowned at the sight of the beaten and obviously raped woman. They didn't have time for antics such as that, though he wasn't about to chastise his men for it.

Not now.

For he understood their needs more than most. He had resisted the temptation of taking advantage of the "comfort women" on offer. He wanted to remain true to his wife, though it was difficult at times, especially when so much flesh was on display before him.

He could take the woman for himself, or perhaps one who hadn't already been spoiled, and fulfill his pent up desires while his men finished the task at hand.

Yet no matter how much he wanted to, the image of his smiling wife always prevented him from pressing forward, from taking advantage of his position, of using captured women held in camps around the newly conquered empire to satisfy his needs.

You're a saint.

He grunted.

And you're going to explode one of these days.

The woman and what might be her son disappeared into the cave, the woman whimpering, the boy screaming and beating his free hand against the soldier dragging him, his protests fading as they were led deeper inside.

"Is that all of them?"

His lieutenant stepped forward. "Yes, sir. We searched the village and the surrounding area and found no one. I'm confident we have them all."

"Good. And the explosives?"

"Ready on your command."

"Excellent. Proceed, Lieutenant, then I want the village burned."

"Won't that raise suspicions? Especially if there are no bodies?"

"It might, but the fact there are no bodies will make people think that they moved on. And with nobody alive, nobody will think to look here for them."

The lieutenant smiled. "An excellent plan, sir."

Kijima ignored the compliment, instead turning on his heel and proceeding down the hill as the warning was shouted, a terrific explosion ripping through the air moments later.

Sealing the fate of the village the Empire hadn't bothered to name.

The Lotus
Tokyo, Japan
Present Day

"You appear to be emptyhanded. You realize we don't take checks."

Akira's men roared with laughter, momentarily drowning out the constant pounding of the bass track on the other side of the insulated walls of the Yakuza boss' inner sanctum. Takashi Kijima forced a smile, his entire body shaking. "I-I've come with something better."

"Better than the millions of yen you owe me?" Akira took an exaggerated look behind Takashi. "I don't see her. Where is she?"

More laughter.

"Have you ever heard of Yamashita's Gold?"

Akira's smile disappeared, and he held up a finger, silencing the room. "It sounds familiar."

"During the Second World War, the Imperial forces stole billions of dollars' worth of gold and other priceless items like artwork and gems. It was all collected in Singapore by General Yamashita, then transported to the Philippines where his command had been transferred. They intended to transport it to Japan, but the Americans prevented that, so they hid it in the Philippines."

"I call bullshit on that, boss."

Takashi's blood drained from his head and he felt faint. Akira leaned forward and shoved his chest, sending him into a nearby leather chair with a thud. One of his men stepped forward holding his phone.

"It says here that Yamashita's Gold was found in 1971 by some guy named Roxas, outside of Baguio City. Apparently, the Filipinos beat the shit out of him until he told them where it was, then the dictator Marcos stole it all."

Akira stared at Takashi. "So, you take us for fools?"

Takashi shook his head, only slightly recovered. An impossibly gorgeous woman walked over and handed him a bottle of water. He smiled slightly and twisted off the cap, downing half of it, life returning within moments. "No, my hiijiisan explained it. That was a secondary hoard. Only a fraction of the treasure. The rest was actually hidden inside a cave in Mindanao, in the south."

"Your hiijiisan? You expect me to believe your great-grandfather knows where billions of dollars of gold is hidden, and yet you can't pay your debts?"

"I can prove it. Or at least prove he could know."

Akira looked at the others. "This should be entertaining."

Takashi reached into his jacket pocket and was immediately surrounded by pistols aimed at his head. He nearly wet himself. "I-I'm just getting an envelope."

Akira waved them off and Takashi removed the envelope and opened it with great difficulty, his hands jerking furiously from the adrenaline coursing through his veins. He finally produced the pages, handing them over.

"What am I looking at?"

"My hiijiisan's military records. He was a captain in the war who served under Yamashita. You can see his last posting was in the Philippines. It's all there."

Akira glanced at the pages then tossed them on the table between them. "That tells me nothing except that an impossibly old man served where there once might have been gold. I see no proof here of a second stash, nor any evidence he could have known about it." He leaned forward, jabbing a finger at him. "You're stalling for time. You think that you can send us off on some foolish errand while you try to figure a way out of your mess." He leaned back in his chair. "I'm tired of this. Do you have my money?"

"No, and I never can." Takashi picked up the pages, carefully folding them then returning them to the envelope. "This is worth billions, and my hiijiisan swears he knows exactly where it is. He's willing to tell you in exchange for clearing my debt and swearing no harm will come to me, my family, or my restaurant."

"The old man doesn't want much, does he? How about I just go beat the location out of him? Then I get this so-called gold, and you still owe me the money."

Takashi paled at the thought of his poor hiijiisan assaulted. "He's approaching one-hundred years-old. He'd rather die than tell you."

"Then I'll beat you until he tells me."

Takashi shook his head. "You don't know him. He will never tell you until he has your word."

Akira grunted. "Then he has it."

Takashi gripped the arms of his chair. "He, umm, wants to meet you. He wants to look you in the eye when you make the promise, to see if he can trust you."

Akira leaped from his chair. "What? My word isn't good enough for some old fossil? I'll meet him! Then I'll kill him! The insolent old fool can keep his gold!"

"Akira!"

Everyone in the room froze, even the irate Akira, as a man emerged from the shadows. How long he had been there, Takashi wasn't sure, but it was clear by the shocked expression on Akira's face, that no one had known he was.

"Father! What are you doing here?"

Takashi felt the room spin for a moment at the realization of who had just made his presence known.

Akira's father.

The oyabun. The head of Akira's entire syndicate of Yakuza. Tens of thousands of men and women swore allegiance to this man as if he were their father. Oyabun literally translated as "foster parent," and no one dared challenge him in any way lest they face death.

Heads around the room were bowed with respect, even Akira straightening himself. Takashi struggled to his feet then bowed, trembling with renewed fear.

The oyabun stepped closer, accompanied by two large bodyguards, finally stopping in front of Takashi. "I came to see my son, and instead find a disrespectful self-centered ignoramus."

"But—"

The oyabun raised a finger. "You know how I hate that word!"

So, that's where he gets it from.

"General Yamashita is a legend, and the fact the Empire amassed an incredible amount of gold during the war is fact. It is also fact that it has never been seen again. I have read about the gold that was found in the Philippines, and it was not nearly enough to be the entire treasure if it is as described." The oyabun turned toward his son. "If you didn't spend so much time playing video games and racing your cars, and instead did some reading about the world around you, you would know this, and recognize that what this man is offering deserves investigation. The wealth that might be found could change everything."

"Yes, Father."

The oyabun faced Takashi. "It would be my honor to meet with your hiijiisan, and discuss his terms."

Mindanao, The Philippines
November 6th, 1944

The screams and cries echoed throughout the cave as the panicked villagers pressed deeper inside, away from the entrance that had collapsed moments before after a tremendous bang unlike anything Juan had heard before. His father held him in one arm over his shoulder, and he assumed had his mother with them as well, complete darkness now enveloping them.

He was wailing along with so many others, never before in his life experiencing such terror. His heart was racing, his ears were pounding, his entire body drenched in sweat, his mouth filled with dust or powder, his eyes burning from the same.

A match flaring behind him caught his attention and the tiny sense of comfort it brought had his wails waning as he and the others focused on it. A makeshift torch was created and the retreat deeper into the cave halted as the one torch was used to find other materials to light, and within minutes, several small fires were burning from scraps of wood and broken apart crates.

A sense of calm took hold, and the village elder pointed toward the entrance. "Someone go check to see if we are indeed sealed inside."

"I'll go," replied someone Juan couldn't see.

"Now, does anyone know of another way out of here?"

Murmurs to the negative rippled through the crowd, and Juan's whimpers returned.

"There's a small hole!" cried the man as he returned. "Come, look!"

Everyone rushed toward the entrance, the settling dust highlighted by a single beam of the fading sun shining through a small opening. The men rushed forward, including his father who handed him off to his silent, trembling mother. He hadn't heard her say a word since they had been dragged into the cave, and he was worried. What he had seen had been wrong. It had been against God's will. It was something only mothers and fathers should do.

There was a word for it, yet that word escaped him.

He just prayed his mother would be her old self soon.

He took her hand then turned to watch the efforts of the men as they attempted to clear away the stone. At first, he had hope, the smaller rocks easily moved, handed from man to man and tossed far enough away to not create yet another barrier to their escape, though hope turned to frustration as it was clear what remained was simply too big to move.

Far too big.

Minutes seemed like hours, and with the sun almost gone, so was their optimism. They weren't getting out of here. His father returned, hugging them both.

"It's no use."

Juan eyed the faint hole then pulled away from his parents' embrace and rushed toward the pile of stone, weaving between the dejected villagers who had struggled for so long, then scrambled up the boulders and to the small hole.

A hole he was convinced he could fit through.

He reached his arms through then pushed with his feet, succeeding brilliantly before he found himself wedged at the shoulders.

"Juan, what are you doing?" cried his father, and he felt hands on his feet.

"I can fit! I know I can! Push me!"

"No, you'll just get hurt."

"You have to let him try, he might be our only hope!" said someone, and he could hear the others were on his side. For they were right, he was their only hope.

"Please, Father, let me try!"

He could hear the sigh behind him. "Very well." His father's hands gently squeezed his ankles. "Let out all your breath, then try to move forward."

"Yes, Father."

He breathed deeply then exhaled as hard as he could, his lungs burning for air, and the moment he wheezed, his father pushed on his bottom, signaling Juan his efforts should begin. He pulled with his hands and wiggled as hard as he could. He was seeing stars, desperate to take a breath, yet he was making progress, progress he might never achieve again if he took in air.

Suddenly he slid forward, his shoulders through, then his torso, then his hips, and he scrambled forward then turned around, staring back in the hole, the glow of a torch revealing his father's elated face.

"Father! I made it!"

"I'm so proud of you, son."

"I'll go get help!" He was about to turn when his father reached out. Juan climbed back inside the narrow opening and took the hand.

"Don't go to the village, understand? And avoid the Japanese. Follow the road, and when you come to the next village, tell them what happened. Tell them to hurry, we don't have much time."

Juan nodded. "You can count on me, Father."

The grip on his hand tightened. "Your mother and I love you. Never forget that, no matter what happens."

Juan's chest tightened, sensing his father expected him to fail.

Yet he wouldn't.

He couldn't.

All the lives of anyone he had ever known depended on him.

And he was determined not to let them down.

Sheraton Cairo Hotel & Casino

Cairo, Egypt

Present Day

"I wish I could see you more often."

Retired Special Air Service Lieutenant Colonel Cameron Leather reached over and ran a finger across his girlfriend's forehead, pushing aside a lock of hair. "You knew what you were getting into when we started dating."

Adelaide Burnett's lips pushed out, displaying a pout that would make any child proud. "I know, but I still don't have to be happy about it."

Leather sighed. "Me neither. You could always quit your job and come with me. You could help run the company."

She gave him a look. "Or you could quit your job and come live with me."

He laughed. "I see your point. You know, things must have been so much easier in the old days."

"What? When women were barefoot and pregnant in the kitchen, waiting for their big man to come home from work so they could dote on them for every waking moment?"

"Exactly!"

"Where's your gun?"

He chuckled. "I didn't say I wanted it that way, I just meant it must have been simpler. Back then, we'd have met, fallen in love, and you'd have dropped everything to follow me around the world."

She stared at him. "I think a little part of you yearns for those days."

He shrugged. "Hey, it was a man's world and I'm a man. But I like my women more liberated. I like to be kept on my toes."

"And I keep you on your toes?"

He grunted. "And then some."

"So, what are we going to do? Eventually, I'll be transferred by Foreign Affairs to some other embassy or consulate somewhere in the world, or your job in the desert guarding a bunch of pimply-faced kids will be finished, then we'll barely see each other. With just an eight hour drive between us, we only see each other once or twice a month."

His chest ached at her words, for she was right. He ran a security company he had created after retiring from the British Special Air Service, pulling in dozens of former Special Forces from various nations to provide security for the rich, famous, powerful—whoever had money to pay his exorbitant fees, and who felt they were truly in danger from the nuts of the world.

Enter Laura Palmer.

He never would have thought a lowly archaeology professor would require his type of security, yet she did in spades. And she was so rich with the inheritance she had received from her late tech entrepreneur brother, that she could afford him.

In fact, she could afford *him*.

She insisted on the best, and that was him. And he didn't mind. He loved the work, and she was yet another woman that kept him on his toes, currently babysitting a group of students at a dig site in southern Egypt. They had come under serious attack by Islamic fanatics, and it had been a bloody, vicious battle to save them.

Too many dead.

The job provided employment for dozens of veterans like him with the physical and mental scars of doing their nations' bidding for years, battling the worst of humanity, while witnessing atrocities and tragedies that would break most.

He gave them structure.

He gave them purpose.

And he'd keep giving them that until the day he died.

Even if it meant being alone.

"What are you saying?"

She wiggled across the bed and into his arms. "I'm not saying anything. I just don't want this to end."

He held her tight, burying his face in her long blond hair, breathing in her scent. "Neither do I."

"Promise me we'll figure this out?"

He closed his burning eyes and squeezed her tighter. "I promise."

Yet he had no clue how they could.

His phone demanded his attention and he let her go, rolling over to grab it off the nightstand.

Speaking of women who keep me on my toes.

He swiped his thumb as he rolled his feet out of the bed, taking a seated position. "Professor Palmer, how are you?"

"I'm good, Cameron. I called the camp and they said you were in Cairo. Sooo, how's Adelaide?"

He smiled. "She's fine."

Adelaide waved at the phone.

"And she says hello."

"Say hello to her for me." There was a sigh. "Now that I know you're with her, I feel terrible for interrupting."

"What do you need?"

"James and I are heading to the Philippines in a couple of hours along with Tommy and Mai."

Leather tensed. "Where in the Philippines?"

Please don't let it be Mindanao.

"Mindanao."

Of course that's where she's going.

"A dangerous place, ma'am."

"I know, which is why I thought we should bring some security."

Leather frowned. "I can't talk you out of it?"

"No, unfortunately this is just too important."

"Is this job-related?"

"Yes. We might have a line on where to find Yamashita's Gold."

"I've heard of that, I think."

"It's the gold the Japanese looted during the war. Worth perhaps hundreds of billions."

His eyebrows shot up. "Really?"

"Yes. So, needless to say, secrecy is important, and unfortunately, it's in Mindanao where there are several active Islamic terrorist groups, if I'm not mistaken."

"You're not."

"So, what do you think?"

"I think you're crazy to go in there, ma'am, but I also know I'll never talk you out of it."

"Can you send a team to meet us in Manila?"

"I'll come myself. I know some good men that are local. Too many Caucasians and we'll attract attention. When will you be arriving?"

"It's a seventeen-hour flight, so let's say twenty-four-hours."

"Very well. I'll be there to meet you."

"You can get there before us?"

"I'm already closer, ma'am."

She chuckled. "Sometimes I forget the world isn't flat." She paused. "Do you really expect trouble?"

"Ma'am, it's the Philippines, which means corrupt government officials are always a problem, but that's just a money thing. Greased palms always get you out of those things. You're coming in on a private jet, so they won't bother you. They'll be too scared you're somebody important who can cause trouble for them. Just don't let anything out of your sight. When we get into the city, it's the normal petty crime stuff you're used to in any third world country. We'll try to minimize your exposure. It's Mindanao that's the problem. We'll try to keep as low a profile as possible, but if we run into trouble, my men are trained for this. We'll have satcoms as well with another team on standby if it turns into a hostage situation. Normally, they kidnap for ransom rather than just kill."

"Now you've got me really nervous."

"I won't lie to you, ma'am, it's a risk, but I also like to practice an overabundance of caution when it comes to my clients' safety."

"And we love you for that. I'll try to put it out of my mind, then. We'll see you tomorrow in Manila."

"Yes, ma'am." He ended the call and turned to Adelaide.

"Now you've got *me* worried."

He grunted. "Just another day in the life of a hero."

She laughed. "And God's gift to mankind?"

He shrugged. "Hey, you said it."

She rose to her knees and pulled him back into the bed, pushing him on his back. "Well, God's gift, how much time do we have?"

"I've got to make a few calls, then maybe a couple of hours."

She straddled him. "Then don't let me interrupt you. I just need a few minutes."

He dialed his second-in-command, Warren Reese, then groaned. "You're evil."

"I'm busy."

He ended the call before Reese could answer, and instead sent a text, each word more difficult to type than the last.

He hit send.

"You've got five minutes."

She moaned. "I don't need it."

He grinned. "I knew there was a reason I liked you."

She stared down at him, lust in her eyes. "Just one?"

He grabbed her breasts. "I can think of two more right now."

Mindanao, The Philippines
November 6th, 1944

Every structure within sight was engulfed in flames, the fields of crops and the jungle lit with an eerie orange glow as embers and smoke drifted high into the night sky. Scores of vehicles had been cycling through the small village for two days, unloading their cargo then continuing farther along the trail as there was no room to turn around until the entire convoy made it through. And their backbreaking work was finally done. The trucks were fully loaded with the personnel he had brought, and everyone but the drivers were once again blindfolded, the canvas backs of the transports closed tight to minimize the usefulness of any peeking that might occur.

For men were curious, and someone was bound to wonder where they had been, and how to get back here. Though none knew what their cargo was, he was certain some suspected. If they had thought it was merely supplies and weapons, they were cured of that error when the villagers were sealed inside.

Why kill an entire village for supplies?

And why leave them alive inside with provisions, and likely explosives they could use to free themselves?

No, he was certain the brighter ones among his men would realize that what was inside were not supplies, not weapons, but something more valuable.

And they would have heard the rumors.

Yet rumors couldn't hurt them if they had no clue where they had been. The confiscated valuables were safe from their curiosity.

Though not that of the drivers.

Despite the fact they didn't know where they were as he had the only map, he couldn't risk any of them perhaps having a sharp memory and a knack for recognizing landmarks that might lead them back.

This was the Empire's future he was protecting, and he couldn't risk it being stolen now, or after a failed attempt to defend the islands.

Freedom could be bought by a captured, tortured soldier, with a secret such as this.

And one life was too insignificant with what a treasure trove such as this could provide for a desperate nation.

He suppressed the frown at the sight of his driver climbing into the lead truck.

He would be dead before the sun set tomorrow, along with all the others.

They just didn't know it yet.

He took one final look at the village as the walls of a once humble home collapsed in on each other, and prayed this wasn't the fate of his homeland should the Americans succeed in their efforts. How many villages, how many towns, how many cities would be razed for what the Empire had done, by foreigners determined to exact revenge. Would the village he had grown up in be burned to the ground, to be reclaimed by nature over time, its history, its memories lost forever?

He hoped not. Surely, some would survive to tell the stories, even if the homes were gone.

He stared up at the hill nearly lost in the dark, and frowned.

Who would remain to tell the stories of this village, of these people?

An unfamiliar ache gripped his chest, and for a moment, a brief moment, he was overwhelmed with regret at what he had done.

But only for a moment.

For the Emperor and the Empire must survive.

No matter the cost.

Kijima Residence

Tokyo, Japan

Present Day

Kijima desperately wanted to stand, to show the proper respect the powerful and terrifying man that now stood before him was due, yet couldn't. He was simply too weak to do so without help.

"Forgive me, Oyabun, but in my state, I cannot rise."

The man, perhaps in his sixties, instead bowed deeply. "It is *I* who is honored to be in your presence, Captain Kijima."

Kijima chuckled then coughed. "It has been a long time since I have been called that." He regarded the man. "I am pleased it is you I am dealing with. I know I can trust your word." He waved a hand toward Akira in the corner. "This younger generation…"

The oyabun smiled slightly. "I understand. I too fear for our future." His face became serious. "I understand you have a proposition for me."

"Yes, Oyabun. You have heard of Yamashita's Gold?"

"Of course. Unlike my son, I am aware of the world outside the video screen."

"Good, good. Then I shall not waste your time. I know where it is, and I am willing to tell you in exchange for your word that my great-grandson's debts will be forgiven, no more protection money will need to be paid, and that he, his family, and business, will be left alone."

The oyabun nodded. "You have my word, provided what you claim is true."

"It is."

The oyabun leaned forward and Kijima's heart raced. "If you are lying to me, old man, I will show your great-grandson no mercy."

"I am not lying."

"I don't believe you are, however, for insurance, we will take him with us just in case." He rose, staring down at Kijima. "And if you are lying, I'll have him skinned alive."

Kijima gripped the arms of his chair, his jaw squaring as he returned the stare. "If you are changing the terms, then so will I."

"What do you mean?"

"I will tell you how to find the gold, but only through Takashi. I will guide you each step of the way, but should he come to harm, you will have nothing."

"Then I will kill you as well."

Kijima shook his head. "My soul died the day I buried that gold, and at long last, my body soon will as well."

Mindanao, The Philippines
November 6th, 1944

Engines roared down the hill, the sound sending Juan scurrying into the trees, hiding behind the largest he could find. The sounds of the jungle never scared him, though the creatures that lay within did.

He shouldn't be out at this hour.

Yet he had no choice.

The fate of all those trapped in the cave depended upon him reaching the next village in time.

His stomach grumbled, and he realized he hadn't eaten since breakfast, beyond a small snack. And he was exhausted. He had been traipsing up and down the hill all day, hauling water to keep everyone fueled in preparation for their ultimate betrayal by what he now realized were evil Japanese soldiers.

His father had been right to be afraid of them.

The sounds of the trucks faded, and he was about to cut through the trees to the road below when he smelled smoke. He returned to the footpath traveled so heavily earlier and spotted a strange orange glow below. He picked his way down the path, the darkness nearly complete under the heavy canopy of trees, then gasped as he emerged into the clearing that was his village.

Had been his village.

Everything was afire.

He rushed toward his home, the heat unbearable as the flames licked at him, and when he reached it, he cried out, the entire structure ablaze, everything he had ever known, everything he had ever owned, inside.

He had to stop it.

He raced toward the river that passed along the southern side of the village, where he had been fetching water all day, and grabbed one of the discarded buckets. He filled it then returned to his home, throwing it onto the flames.

A hiss of protest was all he received in return.

He repeated the process, over and over, and was convinced at one point his efforts were succeeding, until he realized they weren't, any perceived success merely the fact there was little left to burn.

His home was gone.

And he was exhausted beyond anything he could have imagined.

The flames continued their assault, and he found it hard to breathe, the heat unbearable despite the chill of the night. He made for the river, the safest place to be in a fire, he was certain, and spotted his father's small boat. He pushed against the wooden hull, yet it wouldn't move. He threw his shoulder into it and it budged, ever so slightly, toward the water. After several more attempts, he finally had it afloat, and he scrambled inside before the current could capture it. Grabbing the oar, he battled to keep it in place, yet with each stroke, he lost the fight, and soon his home was nothing more than a glow on the horizon.

And eventually even that was gone.

He collapsed in the bottom of the boat, his entire body aching, his stomach sore with hunger, his mouth dry, his exhaustion so overwhelming, the presence of mind to drink from the river was lost to him.

He fell into blissful sleep, his vital task forgotten to him.

Ninoy Aquino International Airport
Manila, The Philippines
Present Day

Takashi entered the packed terminal, his eyes wide, his pulse pounding as sweat beaded on his forehead and upper lip. It wasn't that it was particularly hot, it was the terror gripping him. He had always assumed his hiijiisan would simply tell the Yakuza the location of the gold, then everything would be done.

Never would he have imagined he'd be sent to the Philippines to collect it. He had never left Japan before, and never had any plans to for some time—starting a restaurant, even something as basic as a Japanese take on a pizza joint—was a fulltime job and then some. There was no time or money for travel.

Yet here he was, against his will, with death hanging over his head with every breath he took.

And the dozens of heavily armed soldiers mixed among the travelers wasn't helping his state of Zen.

He spotted Shiro, his assigned escort, and weaved his way through the throngs as they headed to collect their luggage. Shiro handed him a phone.

"Tell the old man that you've made it, and we need to know where to go."

"Okay." Takashi dialed the number for his hiijiisan, and was relieved to hear his voice. "Hiijiisan, it's me. I'm in Manila."

"Are you all right? Have they hurt you?"

"No, I'm fine. They want to know where to go."

"Tell them to get to Cotabato City in Mindanao, then prepare for a drive of several hours and a brief climb. They'll need equipment to clear a collapsed cave entrance."

"Okay, I'll tell them."

"Be careful."

"I will. I'll call you when I'm out of the airport."

"Very well."

He ended the call and handed the phone back, his hands shaking, something they hadn't stopped doing for what felt like days. Shiro took the phone then gripped Takashi's wrist, causing him to wince from the small wound left behind when they had implanted a subdermal tracker. "Calm down or you're going to get us caught."

Takashi nodded, though only shook more. This situation was unlike anything he had ever experienced. He wasn't a brave man. He wasn't used to these stress levels. It had taken everything he had to muster the courage to borrow money from Akira in the first place, yet overconfidence had played a major role in that. He had been certain his restaurant would be a huge success right out of the gate, and it had been, to a point.

He had a steady clientele, lunch and dinners were great, the office crowd enjoying his unique offerings, and he'd already be profitable, making handsome payments to Akira, if it hadn't been for the trick pulled on him.

He would never forget the day the two Yakuza men had arrived after the first week, informing him of the new arrangement. He had protested, though the first sharp word nearly had him soiling himself.

He *definitely* wasn't a brave man.

And even brave men didn't defy the Yakuza.

Not when one owed them money.

And just like that, with the gentle gong announcing a new customer's arrival, all his profits were gone, and then some. He was barely hanging on now, and he was very close to calling it quits and shutting down the business, though he feared that would be not only the end of his dream, but his life as well.

Shiro grabbed their suitcases from the luggage carousel and handed him his. "Go. I'll meet you on the other side. Try to stay calm or you're going to get caught."

I wish he'd stop saying stuff like that.

He drew a deep breath and was about to continue toward customs when a soldier approached. Shiro casually walked away but was blocked by an extended arm. The soldier said something in a language Takashi didn't understand, though the body language and apparent constant anger on the soldier's face suggested he wasn't happy about something. When neither of them said anything, Shiro was pushed back toward Takashi. He glanced at Shiro, who had his hands slightly raised, a smile on his face.

Takashi mimicked him, though from what he was sensing, his facial muscles were twitching fiercely.

This turned him into the focus of the soldier's attention, more Filipino spat at him.

He had to say something. "I-I'm sorry, I don't understand."

The soldier frowned, evidently not understanding Japanese. Another approached to see what was going on, the situation quickly spiraling out of control.

He switched languages. "I speak English, if that helps."

Both soldiers immediately understood, the first snapping his fingers. "Passport."

Takashi passed it over, his hand shaking horribly.

"Why you so nervous?" asked the soldier, handing the passport to his partner who indicated Shiro should hand his over as well.

"I-I'm scared to fly."

The man's eyes narrowed. "Then why you here?"

"Va-vacation."

The soldier jerked a thumb toward Shiro. "With him?"

Takashi's eyes widened. "No. I've never seen him before."

"Then why he grab your arm?"

Shiro finally said something. "He looked like he was about to faint. I was just trying to help."

Takashi nodded a little too quickly. "Yes, that's right. I was feeling a little woozy."

The second soldier eyed them suspiciously, especially the over-confident Shiro. Suddenly his hand darted out and he pulled down Shiro's shirt, revealing part of his chest.

And a portion of the full-body hand-poked *irezumi* tattoos so many loyal Yakuza bore.

The soldier's eyes flared and he stepped back. "Yakuza!"

Everyone in the immediate vicinity froze, then the two soldiers raised the barrels of their rifles at them as more soldiers turned to see what had caused the outburst. Shiro's right hand darted out and grabbed the barrel of the second soldier's Remington R4 rifle, shoving it to the side then pulling it toward him. A shot rang out, missing Shiro, and sending the crowds around them scurrying in panic as his left hand grabbed the butt of the rifle and shoved it up and into the soldier's chin, momentarily incapacitating him.

Shiro spun the weapon around and squeezed the trigger, several rounds hammering the other soldier in the chest. He shoved the second to the ground, releasing the weapon, and grabbed Takashi by the arm, hauling him forward, toward the customs booths. An alarm sounded as soldiers poured into the area, those already there forcing their way through the panicked crowds now rushing the gates.

A line of customs officials attempted a human chain to stop the surging passengers, but failed miserably as they were hopelessly outnumbered. Takashi found himself caught up in the crowd, Shiro's grip on his arm broken. He continued forward, his panicked mind no longer processing what was going on around him. One soldier was dead, another assaulted, and he hadn't been in the country an hour. His face was certainly caught on innumerable cameras, and he was likely moments away from either death or arrest, a possibility that might be worse given where he was.

He spotted the outer doors to the terminal ahead, and felt a surge of hope. If he could get outside with the crowds, and rendezvous with the other Yakuza who had arrived ahead of them, he might just get away with this. Surely, they would have a way to get everyone out of the country, something that didn't involve the airport, then when he was back in Japan, he could go to the authorities and tell them what had happened, and hopefully clear his name.

For he was no murderer.

The Kijima family were not murderers.

A jolt of recently discovered reality cleaved at his stomach, and a wave of nausea swept over him.

Hiijiisan was a murderer. A mass murderer.

It would take time to reconcile himself with that fact. All he could say for certain was that the man Hiijiisan spoke of was not the man Takashi knew.

He had changed.

And today, what had just happened couldn't be allowed to further tarnish the Kijima name. *He* was no murderer.

Determined to prove his innocence—from afar—he pushed through the crowds, spotting Shiro ahead clearing a path.

Then his heart sank.

A row of at least two dozen soldiers rushed the entrance, creating a wall of flesh and firepower as the crowd continued forward. A shot rang out.

A single shot.

And the herd abruptly stopped as if cows in an arrested stampede. More soldiers continued to stream into the area, and Takashi was left wondering what to do. He lowered his gaze in an attempt to blend into the crowd when something pressed into his back. His shoulders slumped and he raised his hands, slowly turning to find a soldier with a bloodied face standing there.

It was over.

Unknown Location, The Philippines
November 8th, 1944

"There's a boy in here!"

Juan groaned as he struggled to open his eyes, the shouts of people around him growing in clarity as he slowly woke. Hands grabbed him and he was lifted into the air, the sound of water crashing around him something he had never experienced before, but had heard of from some of the men who traveled the river to barter the village's harvests.

He finally forced his eyes open and his parched mouth dropped at the sight of waves lapping against the shore, men and women running across golden sand, concerned looks on their faces as they approached, looks that became even more earnest as they caught sight of him.

What's wrong?

He couldn't see his body, too weak to lift his head that tilted precariously back. Finally someone placed a supporting hand under his head and lifted it up so he could see his body, and it scared him. He could finally see why everyone was so concerned.

He was skin and bones, as starved a body as he had ever seen, and his nearly naked form was covered in blisters from what he assumed was the fire.

He was horrifying.

And it terrified him.

"He's been badly burned by the sun," said one of the men as they approached a village that appeared very much like his own. "He must have been drifting for days."

"Bring water and some broth! And some cloths to wash him!" ordered one of the women, her voice reminding him of his auntie.

Auntie!

"Help them," he said, yet it was no use. His voice was a silent whisper and went unnoticed. He had to tell them why he was here, of the tragedy that had befallen his village, and to send help before it was too late.

What had the man said? That he must have been drifting for days?

The thought made him sick.

He had no idea how long his family and friends might survive, though judging from the state he was in, it couldn't be much longer even if they didn't have to deal with the sun.

He was rushed inside a home and placed on a bed, then the men backed off and the women went to work. He was stripped of his clothes and bathed as water was slowly poured into him followed by a thin soup. Life slowly returned to his body, and within a short while, he was sitting up in the bed, eagerly gulping as much water as they could give him along with more of the soup.

"What's your name?" asked one of the women he had heard called Marikit.

"Juan."

"Where are you from?"

"Maliit na Bahay."

Confused looks were exchanged as if they didn't recognize it.

"Small House?" The woman brushed the hair out of his face. "Is that what your village is called? Small House?"

He nodded. "It's up the river."

A man stepped forward. "Do you know the name of the river?"

Juan shrugged. "It's the river. There's more than one?"

The man took a knee. "Son, there are many rivers. Do you know how far up the river? How many days it would take you to go from your village to the ocean?"

Juan shook his head. "No. I've never left the village. I think some of the men might have come to the ocean to trade, but I don't know. Somebody described the ocean to me once, so that must mean someone has been here." His heart hammered and his eyes shot wide. "You mean you don't know where my village is?"

The man shook his head. "No, we've never heard of it."

"But they're all trapped! They're going to die! You have to have heard of it!" Tears flowed and his entire body shook with anguish. How could it be that no one had heard of his home? So many people lived there. How could it be possible?

A gentle hand was placed on his shoulder. "Calm down, now. What are you talking about? What do you mean they're trapped?"

"The Japanese came. They made us carry heavy boxes up the hill and put them in the cave. Then they forced everyone inside, then blew up the entrance and burned our village. I was able to squeeze through a small hole, but no one else. They're all trapped. If you don't help them, they're all going to die."

The man sighed. "Judging by how long you were out there, son, they're probably already dead."

He wailed, then jumped out of the bed and raced for the door, determined to save them himself, but was caught by the man before he made it two steps. He was handed over to the woman who held him tight as he sobbed. The man rejoined the others in the room.

"We have to try and help."

"I agree, but how? I've never heard of the village."

The man shook his head. "Neither have I, but he said it was by a river, and he was in a boat, so it makes sense that he got in the boat and drifted down the river and out to sea. He could have drifted for some time. The mouth of the river isn't far from here. We should send some men up it, to see if we can find his village."

"But there are several rivers that he might have come out from."

"It makes sense that it would be the nearest. Any farther and I can't see him having survived."

"And if you find this village? What are you going to do? If the Japanese did this, then we risk bringing them here if we interfere."

The man sighed, his head slowly bobbing. "The guerrillas."

"What?"

"The guerrillas. If we find the village, we'll let them know. They can deal with it."

"And *you* know how to find them?"

The man gave his challenger a look. "We *all* know someone who knows." He headed for the door. "We must act quickly. If they are indeed trapped, then they might only have days, if that."

Ninoy Aquino International Airport

Manila, The Philippines

Present Day

Acton gripped Laura's hand as they cleared customs. The airport was swarming with armed guards, and the atmosphere seemed tense. He didn't dare ask the customs officer what was going on, having learned long ago that idle chatter in the Third World could make you appear suspicious.

Nobody was happy dealing with customs.

Simply answer the questions in as few words as possible, then hopefully move on.

And they swiftly did, their charter placing them in a different part of the terminal than the normal airlines, the crowds much thinner. As they headed toward the rendezvous point, Acton made it a point to make sure Tommy and Mai were ahead of them where he could see them, already regretting his decision to let them come, though they seemed blissfully unaware of anything untoward happening.

His head was on a swivel for anything out of the ordinary. If security was this tight, something had either just happened, or might be about to happen.

And with his luck, the latter was more likely.

"Something's going on here," muttered Laura.

Acton agreed. "Let's just get out of here before whatever that is involves us."

Laura pointed toward the doors. "There's Cameron."

Acton smiled. "And that's Buwan with him."

"Cameron looks concerned."

"Doesn't he always?"

Laura chuckled. "True!"

"Jim! So happy to see you!" Professor Buwan Bautista rushed forward, giving Acton a thumping hug as Laura gave Leather a gentler one. Acton was certain the former soldier was never pleased with the reception while on duty, but had learned over time to never deny Laura her preferred method of greeting those whom she considered friends.

"And this must be your lovely wife?"

Acton held out his arm toward Laura. "Professor Buwan Bautista, may I present Professor Laura Palmer."

A handshake was exchanged then Tommy and Mai were introduced. More pleasantries were about to ensue when Leather cleared his throat. "There was an incident here earlier. I'd prefer to get some place secure as quickly as possible."

"What happened?" asked Acton.

"Some shooting. We're not sure what's going on, but security has been increased."

Laura frowned. "Does it pose a problem?"

Leather shook his head. "No, this isn't JFK. These things are more frequent here than in the States. Just keep your doors locked and your eyes open."

Laura nodded. "Of course."

Leather led them through the doors and within moments, they were in a large SUV with tinted windows.

Bautista spun in his seat, staring behind them. "Where's your luggage?"

Acton chuckled. "Don't worry, it's being taken to the hotel."

Bautista shook his head. "Unbelievable." He tapped his window. "This looks different."

Leather glanced back at him from the front seat. "Ballistic glass. Unless they have RPGs, we'll be okay."

Bautista's eyes widened as he turned to Laura. "Just how rich are you?"

Laura laughed. "A lady never tells."

Bautista turned to Acton who raised his hands.

"Hey, don't ask me." Acton gestured toward Leather. "He works for her and carries a gun. He's liable to shoot me if I reveal vital intel."

Bautista laughed. "You certainly have changed, Jim."

Acton eyed the man he hadn't seen in nearly a decade. It had been a onetime meeting at a conference in Hong Kong, though they had kept in touch since then on a regular basis. He considered the man more than a colleague, though didn't truly know him that well. He decided to take everything as friendly. "I hope not for the worse."

Bautista appeared horrified. "Oh no! Not at all! That's not what I meant! I just remember the last time we met, you were trying to scrape together enough money to go to Peru. Now you're flying in on a private jet, have a bulletproof vehicle, and I understand are staying at one of the nicest hotels in Manila." He gestured toward Leather and the driver. "Not to mention these guys. They look so terrifying, I swear they could be Delta Force or something."

Leather grunted. "They wish."

Laura leaned over and patted Bautista's arm. "A word of advice, dear, never mistake British Special Air Service for American Special Forces. It tends to upset them and it likely won't end well for you."

Bautista visibly paled. "I'm, umm, sorry if I insulted you, Mr. Man Who Could Kill Me With One Punch."

Leather waved it off. "I'll live." He checked the GPS. "We'll be at the hotel in ten minutes. All the gear we brought, along with the special items we requested, are being delivered to the address Professor Bautista provided. We'll be ready to head out first thing in the morning, if that's still your plan, ma'am."

"It is." Laura took Acton's hand and turned to Bautista. "We'll freshen up, have a nap, then how about we all meet for dinner?"

Bautista brightened. "Absolutely! May I bring my wife?"

"I insist."

"Excellent."

Leather turned in his seat. "I'd recommend the hotel restaurant, ma'am. It's highly rated, and more secure than leaving the premises."

Laura turned to Bautista. "Is that fine with you?"

Bautista's eyes widened. "Eating at the Grand? Absolutely, though I fear my wife will insist on buying a new dress!"

Mindanao, The Philippines
November 11th, 1944

Rodrigo lay on the floor of the cave, his back pressed against the cool wall, gasping for breath, his beautiful wife lying next to him, her head on his shoulder, barely having said anything since she had been brutally violated by the hateful Japanese.

It had been days. At least five, though he couldn't be sure. He was drifting in and out of consciousness so much, he might have lost count. He was beyond hunger, the pangs no longer registering as his body shut down from the lack of water. He had always heard that water was more important than food, yet dismissed it. With a river running past the village, no one ever went truly thirsty, and they always had enough to eat, even if the offerings were usually simple.

His wife always managed to keep him happy in that department, collecting various plants in the jungle to enhance the flavors. He kissed the top of her head and she flinched then groaned.

"Is he back?"

He shook his head. "No."

"Then they must have captured him."

His eyes burned and his chest ached at the thought of what they might have done to him. "Don't lose hope, my love."

"They took all my hope."

He wrapped his arms around her. "I'm so sorry I wasn't there to help you."

"Please, Lord, let me die."

It was a whispered prayer, said aloud, and it broke his heart. Yet he understood. If his son was dead, if everyone he ever knew was dead, if his beloved wife was dead, he too wanted to die. He stared up into the dark, closing his eyes.

Please, Lord, end our suffering.

A long sigh escaped his wife's lips then the heaving of her chest stopped. He felt for signs of life, but he already knew the answer.

She was dead.

Her suffering was over.

A weak cry escaped his lips as all will to live left him.

And it was greeted with silence, all those around him already gone, he and his wife the only ones who had lasted, clinging to the hope that their precious Juan had survived and would return to save them.

He gasped one last time, his head slowly sagging onto his wife's, his suffering on this earth over, his eternity in Heaven earned along with all the others, a smile slowly spreading as he realized he would soon see them all, and Juan, on the other side.

Ninoy Aquino International Airport

Manila, The Philippines

Present Day

"Why is Yakuza here?"

Takashi sobbed, shaking his head as tears flowed down his face and his bloodied nose ran. "I'm not Yakuza! I swear, I'm not Yakuza!"

"You killed one of our men! You murdered my friend!"

Again he vehemently shook his head. "No! That wasn't me! It was the other man! Not me! I swear on my life that I had nothing to do with it!"

Another open-handed smack made contact with his cheek, his ears ringing, the sting overwhelming, yet it was nothing compared to the club that the man's partner had been using. He squeezed his eyes shut in anticipation of its blow, and moments later the violent impact with his stomach had urine flowing freely.

He couldn't take it anymore.

Shiro's last whispered words to him before they were separated left no room for misinterpretation.

"Tell them nothing, or your hiijiisan dies."

Yet he just couldn't take it anymore.

He was not a courageous man, not a strong man. He had never been in a fight in his entire life, had never experienced the pain of a punch, and avoided anything physical that might involve contact.

Sports was not part of his life.

He loved to cook, and the only pain involved in his chosen profession was the sting of raw onions in the eyes, a sliced tip of a finger from a wayward knife, or a burned hand from an inappropriately handled cast iron pan.

All of which one learned to avoid after time.

"Why are you here?"

The demand was relentless, and he doubted they wanted an answer. They merely wanted to torture those who had killed their comrade.

And he didn't blame them. He'd probably want revenge too, but only on the people responsible.

He wasn't.

He was innocent in all this.

"Yamashita's Gold!"

The words were spat, blood, spit, and snot spraying through the air and staining the floor. Another blow was about to be delivered, confirming his theory, when someone tapped on the glass in front of him, the mirror evidently two-way.

And the beating stopped.

The door opened and a man entered, his uniform much more impressive and ornate than the others, clearly someone in charge. The two men who had been beating him for hours snapped to attention and a jerked thumb over the new arrival's shoulder had them out of the room in seconds. He closed the door behind him then positioned a knocked-over chair in front of Takashi, and sat.

"Tell me again why you are here." The voice was calm. Almost gentle. This was a man who knew his prey was already broken.

And he was right.

"Yamashita's Gold. We're here to find it." The confession was gasped out between sobs as Takashi struggled to control his pounding heart, the pain in his stomach and nose unbearable.

"Yamashita's Gold was found by President Marcos almost fifty years ago."

Takashi shook his head. "That was only a small part of it."

The man's eyebrows rose slightly. "And how would you know this?"

"My great-grandfather. He was in the Imperial Army during the war, stationed here under Yamashita. He was responsible for hiding the gold."

The man took a quick breath, his eyes betraying his excitement. "And you have proof of this?"

Takashi shook his head. "No, my great-grandfather has the map. He told the Yakuza that he would guide them to the gold in order to protect me."

"What do they have over you?"

"A large debt. If I lead them to the gold, they will forgive the debt and won't touch my family."

The man pursed his lips. "Perhaps we can come to a deal. *If* you can prove what you say is true." He leaned forward. "You are facing death for murdering one of my men."

Takashi was about to protest when the man held up a hand, cutting him off.

"I don't care if you didn't pull the trigger. You are guilty by association. You may be sentenced to ten or twenty years in prison, but you won't survive it. *That* I can guarantee. A soft one like you. Japanese. You'll be dead within two years, wishing you were within one. But if what you say is true—"

"I swear, it is!"

"—then perhaps we can make a deal. The gold for your life."

Takashi's shoulders slumped with relief. He might yet get out of this. "Then you must let me speak to my great-grandfather."

Belmont Hotel

Manila, The Philippines

Hiroki cursed as he kicked the couch yet again. Akira was going to kill him, and if he didn't, the oyabun would for sure. He had been given command of this mission, a mission that could make them all rich beyond imagination.

But only if they succeeded.

And right now, Shiro was in custody, though more importantly, so was Takashi. Without him, the mission would fail, they wouldn't get the gold, and upon his return, he'd be cutting off more than fingers.

"We have to break them out."

Hiroki looked at one of his men, Koji. "There are hundreds of personnel guarding that airport, and they're in custody. There's no hope in hell of getting them out."

Koji pointed at the laptop, a map showing a red dot indicating Takashi's position, unchanged for hours. "They'll have to move them eventually. When they do, hundreds become maybe a dozen at best. With the element of surprise, we can easily take them."

Hiroki frowned but nodded. Koji was right. They had to be patient.

And ready.

He glanced at the duffel bags of weapons and supplies delivered earlier by their contacts. "We'll have to be ready to act quickly. That means we need to be mobile. The traffic in this city is insane. Let's gear up and get in position."

His phone rang and he answered it. "Hello?"

"What the hell is going on there?"

He gulped at Akira's irate voice. "Sir?"

"Takashi just phoned his hiijiisan. He's told the Filipinos about the gold, and in exchange for putting him on an airplane back to Tokyo, the old man is going to tell them where the gold is!"

Hiroki gulped and stepped over to the laptop Koji was furiously pointing at, the red dot moving. "There was an incident at the airport. Shiro and Takashi were arrested."

"I don't want excuses, I want results! Can you get to him?"

Hiroki shook his head. "Not a chance."

Akira cursed. "You morons stay put. I'll deal with this."

The call ended and Hiroki collapsed into a chair.

"So, did he have nice things to say?"

Hiroki glared at Koji. "What do you think?"

"What are we going to do?"

"Our orders are to stay put. Akira's dealing with it."

"What do you think he's going to do?"

Hiroki sighed. "My guess? Kill the old man now, then Takashi when he arrives in Tokyo."

Parang, Mindanao, The Philippines
November 16th, 1944

Juan was feeling almost normal now. His sunburn was nearly gone, and he was flush with food and drink. The village was much like his own, though the view of the ocean was incredible. He never tired of simply standing at the water's edge and having the waves wash over his feet, the repetitive sound bringing some peace to his tortured soul.

It had been days since the men left to try and rescue his village, and he never lost hope, despite the others tempering his expectations. He heard the whispers, saw the stolen glances, overheard the adults talking at night when they thought he was asleep.

Everyone thought they were dead. It had been too long.

And they were right if the men sent had failed. Yet if they hadn't, if they had found the village, they might have saved those trapped inside the cave. It was possible. They could pass food and water through the opening he had used to escape to keep them alive while they sought the guerrillas mentioned by the man he had learned was Marikit's husband Gabriel.

It was all plausible, and his mind had so many invented images that he had convinced himself it must be true, for surely God wouldn't let him imagine such wonderful things if they weren't.

Shouts at the other end of the beach had him turning to see a boat approaching, Gabriel at the prow along with the other two who had gone with him. His heart leaped as a smile spread. He raced toward them as several of the men from the village ran into the water to help haul the small boat ashore.

He skidded to a stop in front of Gabriel, his smile wide. "Did you find them? Did you see my parents?"

Gabriel frowned and Juan's heart sank, his knees shaking as he already knew what the man was going to say. "I'm sorry, Juan, but we didn't find them."

Marikit approached, putting an arm around Juan as sobs racked his body. "What happened?"

"We traveled upriver for days. Every village we reached, we asked of Juan's, and no one had heard of it. It was pretty clear we were on the wrong river, but he might have traveled farther than we thought. We kept going, but eventually it didn't matter. We never found any burned or abandoned villages, and one morning a Japanese patrol spotted us and fired. We managed to escape downriver, and decided it was best to return." He knelt in front of Juan, placing his hands on the boy's shoulders. "I'm sorry, Juan, but if they haven't been found by now, then I'm afraid there's no hope."

"But—but, maybe someone else found them. Maybe they're out there looking for me!"

Gabriel shook his head. "Son, if the Japanese did what you described, then there's nobody left to find them. I'm so sorry, but you're going to have to accept that they are now in Heaven, waiting for you to join them one day, long from now. They'll always be with you as long as you keep them in your heart."

Juan's shoulders shook. "Will I forget them?"

Marikit knelt before him. "In time, perhaps."

The very idea was crushing. "I-I don't want to forget."

"Then you must force yourself to remember. Repeat the stories they told you every night, tell us of what life was like with them and in your village."

Gabriel nodded. "You should write them down. Write down everything you know, so that when you are older, you can read your words and remember."

Juan's shoulders slumped. "I don't know how to write."

"Then we'll make sure you learn."

A glimmer of hope reentered Juan's soul. Perhaps he could keep his parents alive in his head, and never forget them or those of the village. If he were indeed the lone survivor, then he had a responsibility to keep those memories alive so that the world would never forget those he had loved so much, and who had loved him.

His heart ached at the thought.

"What's wrong, dear?"

His chin dropped to his chest, and sobs racked his body. "If they're gone, who will love me?"

City Garden Grand Hotel

Manila, The Philippines

Present Day

Acton popped a slice of mango in his mouth, savoring every chew. He swallowed and turned to Laura sitting to his right, Mai and Tommy occupying the other two seats at the table in their hotel suite.

"Why does mango never taste quite as good back home?"

Laura flipped through something on her phone. "Because these mangos probably came from a tree fifty meters from here, and your mangoes back home from another continent."

He picked up another slice. "You might be right." He popped it into his mouth.

"I always am."

He rolled his eyes for the benefit of the kids.

Mai Trinh giggled. "Manila kind of reminds me of back home."

Laura put down her phone. "Do you miss it?"

Mai shrugged. "Sometimes, terribly, but Maryland is my home now. I know I can never go back."

Tommy took her hand. "Maybe someday."

She shook her head. "As long as the communists are in charge, I can't, and they'll never let go of power."

"Oh, you poor dear." Laura leaned over and gave Mai's shoulder a squeeze. "I'm so sorry. I wish there was some way you could see your family."

"It would be nice, but at least with the Internet and cellphones, I can chat with them."

Acton frowned. "Using burner phones on a schedule I guess is better than nothing. Twenty years ago you'd be lucky to have that."

Tommy finished the last bite of his breakfast, leaning back in his chair and rubbing his stomach. "Maybe things will relax at some point and they'll be able to get visas to come visit, or at least get out of the country, and you could meet them. Some place like here or Australia."

Laura smiled. "I like that idea. And if it's ever a possibility, you let us know. We'll pay for all the flights and hotels. After all, if it weren't for us, you'd still be back in Vietnam with your family."

Mai's eyes glistened. "It wasn't your fault. I don't want you to ever think that."

Laura squeezed her hand. "I'm sorry, I didn't mean to upset you. You're right, it was the Vietnamese government's fault."

Acton cleared his throat. "Don't forget the Russians."

Laura chuckled. "How could I?"

Tommy grinned. "Soviet Union Two-Point-Oh!"

Acton jabbed a finger at him. "You're learning!"

A knock at the door had Tommy waving off Acton. "I'll get it."

"Remember to check first."

Tommy nodded and headed for the door, Bautista and Leather entering after the required peephole check.

"Buwan! Good morning!" Acton waved at the table. "Did you want us to order you some breakfast?"

Bautista shook his head. "No, thank you. My wife cooked up a storm this morning. I think she's still buzzing from dinner last night."

Laura smiled. "It was a pleasure to meet her. A very lovely woman."

He dropped into a chair in the sitting area. "More than I deserve."

"Cameron, if I know you, you've already eaten and are impatient to get underway."

Leather grunted. "You know me so well, ma'am."

Bautista gestured toward Leather. "I was talking to your security chief and he's informed me that all of my carefully laid plans have been changed."

Laura's eyes narrowed. "Oh? Why's that?"

Leather responded. "Too dangerous."

"How so?"

"It involved driving to our destination. I've had my local contacts make alternate arrangements."

Bautista shook his head. "I had planned a nice drive to the coast, a ferry to Mindanao, then another drive across the island. It would take a couple of days, but you would have seen a lot of the country. Very beautiful."

Laura smiled. "I have no doubt, but Cameron has his reasons, I'm sure."

Leather defended his position. "The planned route would see us traveling for too long through MILF territory."

Tommy snorted.

Acton grinned, but still admonished the young man. "Get your mind out of the gutter. He means the Moro Islamic Liberation Front."

Tommy rolled his eyes. "You'd think if you're going to pick a name for your super-evil organization, you'd at least Google it first."

"Why?" asked Mai. "Does MILF mean something?"

Tommy leaned over and whispered in her ear.

She blushed, then giggled.

Then swatted him. "How do you know that?"

It was his turn to blush.

Laura swatted Acton. "And how do *you* know that?"

Acton's grin spread. "I'm sure from one of my students."

"Riiight." She returned her attention to a stoic Leather. "So, what are the new plans?"

"I had a plane chartered last night to take all of the equipment we brought, as well as all of Professor Bautista's equipment to Cotabato City on Mindanao. That's about half a day's travel to the site. We're still in MILF"—he gave Tommy a look—"territory, but for far less time than originally scheduled. I've sent two of my local hires with the equipment to guard it and arrange transport for when we get there, since we won't be taking the vehicles arranged by the professor. They've also booked several rooms at a hotel that will act as a basecamp if it becomes necessary."

"Seems prudent."

"Thank you, ma'am. I have another charter waiting to take us all to Cotabato. It's only a couple of hours in the air. We can be there before noon, and on the road right away if you want."

Bautista frowned. "So expensive!"

Leather didn't look at him. "Ma'am, my standing orders are to not concern myself with expense when it comes to protecting you and your people."

Laura waved her hand. "You're right. Don't worry about it." She turned her attention to Bautista. "I was looking forward to seeing more of your lovely country, but Cameron is right. This is a much safer way to travel. And, frankly, we are high-risk targets. If word got out who we are, we could attract unwanted attention."

"You mean because of your fabulous wealth?"

Laura laughed. "I meant high-profile foreign academics."

Acton rose. "And it's not exactly a secret what you've been searching for all these years. It doesn't take a genius to put two and two together, and someone might just decide to arrange a little hostage-taking in exchange for a few million."

Bautista shook his head. "They should never have started paying the ransoms. Once these people realized there was a chance of getting paid, kidnapping went through the roof here."

Acton sighed, dropping onto the couch opposite Bautista. "Yup. We don't negotiate with terrorists, but here's the guy who will. How many ordinary people have died because Western governments keep paying for the rich and well-connected?"

Bautista threw his hands up then slapped them down on his knees. "Well, I'm not here to solve the world's problems, I'd just like to solve one of its mysteries. And don't worry, Laura, you'll still see the country. Where your Mr. Leather has us going will still mean travel by vehicle." He rose. "In fact, the very notion of being there in a few hours has me giddy. We could be at the cave before the day is out!"

Laura rose. "Thanks to our protector."

Leather bowed his head slightly. "The sooner we're in, the sooner we're out."

She patted him on the arm as she passed. "You worry too much."

"I'm paid to worry. We should be fine as long as we keep as low a profile as possible."

Bautista agreed. "Things have calmed down there quite a bit since the plebiscite. Everything should be fine."

Acton regarded Leather, noting he wasn't packing. "And if the shit hits the fan, how do we defend ourselves?"

"I've hired three locals, highly recommended. They're former Light Reaction Regiment."

Bautista's eyes widened. "Ooh! They're like your Delta Force."

Leather grunted. "I would have said SAS."

Laura smiled. "Of course you would. So, you haven't worked with them before?"

"No, but people I trust have. They're licensed here as private security, so they have permits to carry weapons. We're well-equipped, and if anything goes wrong—"

"Permits be damned?" suggested Tommy.

"Exactly. Someone will toss me a weapon, and I'll be in the fight."

"Toss me one too," said Laura.

"Me too," agreed Acton. "We can't let all that training you've been giving us go to waste." He turned to Bautista. "So, once we get there, what do you expect to find?"

Bautista sat back down, the eagerness of a child on his face. "I've studied the writings left behind by Juan before he died. Unfortunately, they're the words of a child of ten, many based on fading memories, most with little to do about the events of that day. He was trying to preserve the memory of his people."

Laura wiped a tear from her eye. "It was heartbreaking what he wrote."

Bautista's eyes glistened. "It was." He took a moment to gather himself. "I expect we'll find evidence of a burned, abandoned village, long grown over. There should be a river on one side, long-neglected rice paddies on the other, and a mountain or hill nearby—something high enough that required a short climb from the village, and that would have the possibility of caves. We'll make our way up to it, then search the area for any evidence of a collapsed entrance."

Laura frowned. "I suspect if we do find it, what will be inside will be heartbreaking."

Bautista agreed. "If the story is true, we will find the bodies of perhaps hundreds of men, women, and children inside, who will have taken days to die." He closed his eyes for a moment. "One of our top priorities once the site is confirmed will be to attempt to identify then bury the bodies with the dignity and honor they deserve. Once that is completed, we can begin to catalog the treasure."

Acton put an arm around Laura. "I was reading about that Roxas guy on the flight over. "You're convinced he didn't find the entire treasure?"

"Not the entire treasure, no. Whether he found what he claimed or not, I don't know, though there are stories even Marcos claimed to have found it, and it was the reason he was so rich."

Laura's eyes narrowed. "I thought he was rich because he stole billions from your country?"

Bautista's head bobbed. "Oh, he did, absolutely, but some claim he himself said he was worth as much as a trillion dollars, and that could only be explained by Yamashita's Gold."

Tommy's eyes bulged. "Do you really think it's worth that much?"

Bautista shook his head. "Not at all, though it could be worth hundreds of billions. Remember, they looted all the wealth they could get their hands on from Southeast Asia. We're talking the treasuries of governments, bank holdings, private citizens, art galleries, museums. They took it all, much like the Nazis did in Europe."

Acton winked at Tommy. "We've heard something about that." He turned to Bautista. "Do you think Marcos did find at least some of it, or was he just grandstanding?"

"I think if he said it at all, it was merely boasting. He wasn't a very honest man." He sighed. "I don't know why we keep choosing leaders like that." He shrugged. "Macho culture, I guess, though we're not the only ones who do it. Look at Russia."

"Soviet Union Two-Point-Oh?" offered Mai.

Bautista smiled, poking a finger toward her. "I like that. You should trademark it."

"Oh, I think I might have heard it from someone." She leaned forward. "Umm, who gets to keep the gold when you find it?"

Bautista shrugged. "Not sure. I'll worry about that if and when we find it."

Acton's chest tightened. "Buwan, have you thought about what you'll do if you find it?"

Bautista's eyes narrowed. "What do you mean?"

"I mean, we're talking about possibly hundreds of billions of dollars' worth of gold. It would have taken a large convoy to transport it there. How are you going to get it out of there without attracting unwanted attention?"

Bautista's face slackened. "I, umm, hadn't thought of that."

Tokyo Narita Airport

Narita, Japan

Takashi adjusted the facemask he had retrieved from his carry-on, hoping to cover as much of his broken nose and black eyes as possible, yet remaining inconspicuous was difficult. He was in extreme pain. He was certain he had at least one cracked rib from the brutal assault laid on him by the Filipino soldiers, and was weak from barely having eaten or drunk anything in almost a day.

He couldn't wait to get home and just lie in bed for a week.

And perhaps visit a hospital.

"Remove your mask, please."

Takashi's heart raced as he handed his passport and plane ticket over to the customs official before moving the mask so many of his fellow Tokyo denizens wore to avoid pollution and disease.

"What the hell happened to you?"

He had rehearsed his answer. "I was mugged in Manila."

The man examined his computer screen. "It says you just left here yesterday." He eyed Takashi for a moment. "I guess I don't blame you for coming right back. Are you okay?"

Takashi wanted to tell him everything, yet that would likely get him and his hiijiisan killed. "I'll live."

The man handed him back his documents. "Well, I'd go see a doctor if I were you. You look like hell."

Takashi nodded. "I will, thank you."

He dragged his ass toward the exit and the taxis, wishing he had his cellphone with him. It was the only thing the Filipinos had confiscated. The rest of his luggage—pre-approved by his Yakuza captors—had been returned to him.

I wonder what happened to Shiro.

He didn't care, though he suspected as the triggerman, his beating had been far worse, and likely would end with him found in an alley somewhere. Dead.

Good.

He was almost at the doors when a man stepped in front of him, blocking his path. He handed him a cellphone.

"I believe you have a phone call to make."

Takashi's eyes widened briefly, his heart racing as he recognized the man as Filipino, or at least not Japanese.

This was where he had to fulfill the other end of the bargain Hiijiisan had made with the man in Manila.

He took the phone and dialed his great-grandfather, his nurse answering then handing over the phone. "Hello, Hiijiisan, it's me. I'm in Tokyo."

"Are you safe?"

"I think so. There's a man here with me now. He wants the location."

"I have the map with the location here with me now. We'll have to make a copy. I can't give it to them. The oyabun's men will want it as well. You'll have to come here and take it to make copies."

Takashi smiled slightly at the ancient way of thinking. "You're thinking like it's fifty years ago. Is your nurse there?"

"Yes."

"Put her on."

The voice changed to the nurse attending his hiijiisan for so many years. "I need a favor. Does he have a map?"

"Yes. In his lap."

"Okay, I need you to send me a photo of the map, in the highest resolution possible, to this number."

"Just a second."

The phone vibrated a few moments later and he brought up the image, zooming in on the proverbial X marking the spot, satisfied the resolution was detailed enough.

"Did you get it?"

"Yes, I did. Thank you. Tell him I'll call him soon."

"Very well."

He ended the call and handed the phone to the man who examined the photo then walked away, saying nothing. He took a moment to collect himself, again wishing he had his own phone. He scratched at the tracker in his arm, wondering how he would rid himself of it, or if he even should with his Yakuza business still unsettled.

He checked his watch and smiled slightly as he noticed his hand was steady.

Two men rapidly approached, coming to a halt directly in front of him.

"Akira wants to see you. Now."

His entire body trembled.

Ninoy Aquino International Airport

Manila, The Philippines

Colonel Ramil Ocampo stared at the image on his phone just sent by their man in Tokyo, his heart drumming hard at the possibilities it represented. Could what the young man had told him be true? In his inexpert opinion, the map appeared genuine. He could think of no reason why Takashi would have made up such a story, and even if he had, how would he have such a detailed map ready to go?

It made no sense.

His man from the embassy had intercepted Takashi at the airport, observed the phone call, then sent the result of it to him immediately. In fact, Takashi was likely still waiting for a taxi at the airport, the intel was so fresh. They had also taken away his cellphone, so unless he had made a call from a phone on the plane, no one would have had time to prepare a fake map.

And why were the Yakuza here?

With the same story.

Shiro, their shooter, after almost a full day of beatings had spilled everything eventually. They always did. Sometimes the confessions were simply what the prisoner thought his men wanted to hear, other times they were genuine. It was often difficult to tell which was the case, but in this instance, both confessions matched. The only difference was the swiftness in which it was obtained.

Takashi was far weaker, and far less motivated to keep his tongue.

Shiro was definitely Yakuza. His prints had been run through Interpol to confirm it, though he didn't need that to know what his eyes already told him, the full-body tattoos including genitalia a dead giveaway.

Added up, it meant Takashi was either telling the truth about his great-grandfather knowing where Yamashita's Gold was, or he was lying not only to him, but the Yakuza as well.

A very dangerous notion.

For a very weak young man.

He couldn't see Takashi having the balls to lie to the Yakuza about something like this, and couldn't believe the boy's own great-grandfather would lie and put his own descendant at risk.

No, something was going on here, and though he had heard the rumors that Marcos had confiscated Yamashita's Gold, he was also well aware that it was found outside Baguio City.

Nowhere near where the map indicated.

Again matching the story Takashi had told.

He leaned back in his chair, staring at the map, shaking his head.

Why did it have to be in Mindanao?

Any other place in the country would have been better than Mindanao.

It meant either paperwork or secrecy. Paperwork he couldn't risk. If the wrong people found out why he wanted to go into a semi-autonomous region of the country with heavy equipment, he'd lose any claim to the find. But secrecy meant military, and though he commanded a good number of troops at the airport, he didn't have the equipment to stage an operation in Mindanao.

Especially a clandestine one.

He needed help.

And he could think of only one person who might help him, though that person would destroy him should this prove to be a complex ruse.

You have to pretend to be skeptical.

He grunted.

You are skeptical.

Yet he couldn't risk not investigating. He'd be a fool not to.

And his cousin, whose senior position had given him his job here, was no fool, nor tolerated them.

He would have to approach him carefully, claiming to believe he didn't think it was true, yet convince him they couldn't possibly ignore it in the off chance it was.

He printed off three copies of the map, securing one of them in his cabinet, folding the second tidily into his pocket, then put the third in his briefcase before heading out the door.

"Where will you be, sir, if anyone is asking?"

"National Headquarters. Fort Bonifacio."

The Lotus

Tokyo, Japan

Takashi was confused and embarrassed. He was sitting in a large leather chair at Akira's club with a buxom beauty in his lap tending to his face, and though she was wearing a nurse's uniform, he wasn't certain it was anything more than a cosplay outfit, leaving her qualifications in question.

And his nether regions reacting involuntarily.

"Somebody likes his nurse."

He blushed, though with how red his face currently was, he hoped no one noticed.

She gave him a little peck on the nose then grabbed it between two fingers. "Ready?"

His eyes widened. "For what?"

She jerked his nose and he screamed. "To set it."

His eyes filled with tears, but the pain quickly faded, and the ache that had dominated his face settled noticeably. "So, you really are a nurse?"

She patted his cheek. "Nope. But I just watched a YouTube video on how to do it." She squirmed out of his lap. "That pretty face of yours will be fine eventually." She pointed at his stomach, an area she had seductively looked at earlier, an examination he now realized had been a precursor to some heavy Googling. "You're going to need to see a doctor, though. I'll get some tape for your ribs, but you might have internal bleeding."

Akira, watching the display with some amusement, held up his glass, another beauty quickly emerging from the shadows to refill it. "He'll see a doctor when we have the old man's gold."

His "nurse" shrugged. "He could be dead in a couple of days if he's bleeding. And the pictures I saw kind of look like what he's got."

"Not my concern. If he hadn't got himself caught, he wouldn't be in his current predicament."

The phone Akira had handed him upon his arrival rang. He had been ordered to call his hiijiisan, but though he was home, the nurse who attended him had stepped out, so there was no one to send him the map again.

Akira pointed at the phone. "Answer it."

Takashi grabbed it and swiped his thumb. "Hello?"

"Hello, sir, it's your hiijiisan's nurse. Is he right? You want me to send another photo of the map?"

"Yes, please."

"Give me a moment then." The phone beeped a few seconds later and he checked to confirm the map was there. "I re-sent it. Did you get it?"

"Yes, thank you."

"Try not to lose your phone again."

He didn't bother correcting her, and instead ended the call. He handed the phone to Akira. "Here's the map."

Akira grabbed the phone eagerly, then with a few taps, had the image displayed on a large screen on the wall. He joined his henchmen to stare at it, Akira bringing up Google Maps on another screen, zooming in on the area in question. He turned to Takashi. "It would appear your hiijiisan wasn't full of shit after all."

"I told you he was telling the truth." Takashi glanced toward the door. "Can I go now? I don't feel so well."

Akira shook his head. "No. You will be my guest until we confirm the gold is real."

Takashi's chest tightened. "But that wasn't the deal!"

"I'm changing the deal. My father may trust the old man, but I don't. *If* we find the gold, you will be released and the agreement the oyabun made will be honored. If not, I will personally skin you alive, and force your hiijiisan to watch before I cut his heart out."

Philippine Army National Headquarters
Fort Bonifacio, Manila, The Philippines

"I'm busy, Ramil. What do you want?"

Colonel Ramil Ocampo suppressed his desire to put his cousin in his place, yet he owed him everything. Ten years ago he might have belted him for showing him the disrespect on display at this moment, but that was then, and this was now.

And now, he owed his cousin everything. If it weren't for him, he wouldn't have his job along with the money and power it brought.

Not to mention the opportunities, like the one stumbled upon today.

"I need to speak to you alone. It's important."

Vice Commander of the Philippine Army, Major General Dante Cruz, sighed heavily, as if humoring a child, then flicked his wrist, the staff quickly scampering out of the room, the door closing. Ocampo scanned the room to make certain there were no windows that prying eyes might be peering through, then placed his briefcase on a nearby table. He rolled the tumblers with his thumbs, dialing in the code. He snapped the case open then pulled out the folder with the map.

"There was an incident at the airport yesterday."

"So I heard. If you don't get your shit together, I'll have to replace you, whether you're my cousin or not."

"Well, I think you'll be eating those words when you hear what I have to say."

Cruz sat in his chair and leaned back, folding his arms. "What do you think you've found this time?"

Ocampo cringed, having forgotten in his excitement this wasn't the first time he had been here with intel he had stumbled upon that he thought might impress his higher-ranked cousin.

All had proven false.

Yet this time, he had physical evidence, not just the false confession of some innocent soul.

"This time it's different."

"Of course it is."

Ocampo held up his hands, conceding his cousin's skepticism as valid. "Fine, you're right, I've been off in the past, but let me explain. This time it really is different." He held up the map without explaining it. "And this time I have proof."

Cruz's eyes narrowed. "What's that?"

"Let me explain." Ocampo took a seat opposite his cousin. "Yesterday, one of my men was killed. We arrested two suspects, both Japanese. One was Yakuza, the other we believe a hostage of theirs.

During interrogation, the Yakuza member confessed they were here to retrieve Yamashita's Gold."

Cruz rolled his eyes, his finger pointing at the door. "Get out! I don't have time for this bullshit!"

Ocampo refused to budge. "You'll listen to me, you arrogant fool, or I'll tell your wife what you've been doing with your secretary every Tuesday night."

Cruz's eyes widened. "How the hell—"

"I'm no fool. Now, are you going to listen or what?"

Air blasted through Cruz's lips before he settled back into his chair. "Fine. Yamashita's Gold. Which has already been found, or never existed."

"As I was saying, he claimed that's why they were here. He claimed that the other man's great-grandfather was a Japanese soldier during the war, and was stationed here. He headed the team that hid the gold, and has the map showing where it is."

Cruz sighed. "Right, and I'm sure an X marked the spot, and after all these years, he never bothered to come back and retrieve some of it."

Ocampo waved the map again, still not showing it to the arrogant piece of shit sitting across from him that he so desperately needed right now. "Tell me this. Why would a known Yakuza member—we ran him through Interpol—be traveling with an innocent man, both with the exact same story? If it wasn't true, why *that* story? It's so completely unbelievable, that it would be ridiculous to have rehearsed it. You'd come up with something more plausible, like we're here on vacation, or business, or something else. You'd never come up with Yamashita's Gold."

Cruz grunted a concession, but said nothing.

"And, I spoke to the guy's great-grandfather, and he confirmed the story, and we struck a deal. I'd return his great-grandson, and when he arrived in Tokyo, he'd send me the map. I had a contact at the Embassy meet him at the airport, and the exchange was made." He waved the map again. "This was texted to me a short while ago. There is no way some hundred-year-old man came up with a fake this detailed in the hours it took for his great-grandson to return."

"What is that you keep waving about?"

"The map to the exact location of the bulk of Yamashita's Gold." He handed it over to his cousin, the moment of truth about to transpire. He might be about to lose his job, move forward in the retrieval of untold riches, or be killed so his cousin could keep everything for himself.

Cruz examined the map carefully, shaking his head. "Why did it have to be Mindanao? And that particular area!" He sighed. "That area is crawling with MILF terrorists. We can't safely conduct an operation there without drawing attention to ourselves." He leaned back, once again folding his arms. "I think you're being had."

Ocampo shrugged. "Perhaps, but what if it's true? Can you imagine how much gold there could be?" He lowered his voice. "We'll be rich. Richer than Marcos was. We could buy anything we wanted." He leaned closer. "You could be the next president."

Cruz's cheek twitched with the hint of an ambitious smile. "You're right. Even if there's the remotest chance this is true, we can't ignore this.

But we need to keep this quiet. If word gets out, the place will be swarming with people. Who knows?"

"Besides the prisoners, only two of my men, though they only heard the initial claim. I personally finished the interrogation on the Yakuza member once I heard what his hostage had to say."

"Can they be trusted to keep their mouths shut?"

"I already promised them ten million pesos each if we find anything. They'll keep quiet."

Cruz frowned. "You're forgetting something rather obvious."

Ocampo's eyes narrowed and his heart picked up a few beats. "What?"

"The Yakuza."

"We have him. He won't be a problem."

Cruz shook his head, rolling his eyes. "Do you really think that the Yakuza would send only one man? They're already here, I can guarantee it. And as soon as their hostage was captured by you, I have no doubt they got their hands on this map the same way you did." He jabbed a finger on the X marking the gold's location on the map. "They are either there, or on their way there. I guarantee it."

Ocampo cursed. His cousin was right, it was something he hadn't considered. "Then we need to get moving."

"We need eyes in the area. I've got a rapid response team at Camp Navarro. I can have them inserted in the area, and with drones, we can get some shots of the site, see if anyone is there."

"And if there is?"

"We'll have to eliminate them."

"And if there isn't?"

"Then we'll need to figure out a way to mount a massive recovery operation without the locals knowing about it."

"How could we possibly do that?"

Cruz stared at the map. "We're going to need some sort of distraction."

Kiangan, The Philippines

June 30th, 1945

They had lost.

Or at least they would shortly. The Imperial Army was holding on to a small sliver of land in the northern Philippines, but their defeat was inevitable. The Americans had long since continued their inexorable march toward Japan, content to keep what remained of the Japanese contingent on the archipelago contained.

They were no threat now.

Yamashita stared at the map, shaking his head, muttering insults and curses at the Americans and the gods for allowing such a thing to occur. Kijima was giving the general as much space as he could in the confines of their bunker, though it was proving fruitless.

Yamashita spun on his heel then paused as their eyes met. "You shouldn't be here."

Kijima wasn't sure what to say. "Where do you think I could serve you best?"

"Far away from me." Yamashita lowered his voice. "You and I alone know the locations of the gold. If we're both killed, the Mindanao and Baguio City hoards will be lost forever. The Emperor will never be able to finance the war effort."

Kijima didn't bother commenting on the likelihood of the war's outcome turning enough for his countrymen to ever return here to retrieve the gold. Though the general was correct. The confiscated gold belonged to the Japanese government now, and even if they lost the war, they might one day retrieve it and help rebuild what would be a crippled country.

The gold that had already been loaded onto ships in Mindanao had been transported to the north safely, then offloaded, as there was no chance of the ships reaching Japan or any other territory they still held. Another cave system outside of Baguio City had been located and filled with the holds of the ships, the entrance sealed. The entire operation had been carried out by their men—ignorant as to the mission—with no locals aware of what was going on.

It was barely a fifth of the treasure collected, but significant enough that should anyone find it in the future, they would assume it was the entirety of that which had been confiscated from Southeast Asia.

Mindanao was the real prize, and no one but the general and himself knew its location.

And the general was right.

They couldn't be in the same place together.

"You should leave, General. I will remain."

Yamashita shook his head. "I have never abandoned a command, and I'm not about to start now. I shall remain until the end."

Kijima lowered his voice. "General, surely you agree there is no hope. If you remain, you'll either die, or be captured by the Americans and tortured."

Yamashita sighed, his lips pursed. "I will remain and face the end with my men. It is the only honorable thing to do." He put a hand on Kijima's shoulder. "You must leave now if you have any hope of reaching the coast. There will be a submarine waiting for you. I want you on it. Report the location of the hoards when you arrive home. The very survival of the Empire may depend upon it."

Kijima shook his head. "I cannot abandon you."

"Your loyalty does you honor, Captain, but this is my final order to you. I expect you on the submarine." The hand was removed. "Dismissed." Yamashita turned his back on him, returning to the map he had been examining earlier, leaving Kijima to stare at him for a moment.

The decision had been made.

He had no choice.

To disobey his commander's order would be disgraceful.

He snapped to attention and saluted. "It has been an honor, General!"

Yamashita turned and acknowledged the salute, his expression grave, inevitable defeat and death in his eyes. The great leader, the Tiger of Malaya, the man who had once done such great things for the Empire, returned to his maps, and Kijima left the bunker, joining a group of elite soldiers who would take him to the coast and what was likely the last transport that would ever leave this wretched land.

And as he passed his brave brothers left behind to fight the vicious Americans, he wondered if they would be treated by their conquerors better than his men had treated their own prisoners of war. It was a brutal business, this war, yet he had no regrets. He had answered the rallying cry and done his duty as best he could.

They had done it to save Asia, to save not only Japan, but all their fellow Asians from the Europeans and Americans. It was evident that the whites were determined to carve up Asia as they had Africa and the Americas, and if they weren't stopped here and now, all Asian societies would be subjected to white rule, their cultures suppressed, their way of life destroyed.

Japan had decided it must be stopped, and the only way to do so was to take all of Southeast Asia under its wing and protect it from itself.

And now they had failed.

The Americans and Europeans would move in, carve up the spoils of war, and Asian culture, Japanese culture, would die, replaced with the white man's idea of civilization, thousands of years of tradition suppressed and dismissed.

His heart wept at the thought as he finally understood that the general was right. If there was any chance at victory, the Emperor must know of the fortune hidden in these islands he had called home for the past three years.

For the whites had to be stopped from destroying the most ancient cultures of the world.

Cotabato Airport

Cotabato, Mindanao, The Philippines

Present Day

Acton stepped down onto the tarmac, the sun already baking the ground, waves of heat thrown back at the air in protest. He didn't mind the temperature, it was the humidity that always got him. Throw him in the middle of the Egyptian desert? No problem. It was dry. But here? He was already having difficulty.

"Holy crap! Talk about a sauna!"

Bautista slapped Tommy on the back. "You'll get used to it, my friend. Just stay hydrated."

Tommy's Adam's apple bobbed as he did just that, handing the bottle over to Mai who appeared none the worse for wear, her Vietnamese upbringing preparing her well.

Acton took a swig of water and offered the bottle to Laura who waved it off.

"I'm good."

He regarded her for a moment, her British complexion standing out brilliantly, a large sunhat protecting her face. "Do you ever sweat?"

She winked. "Sometimes."

He grinned.

Hails from the small terminal had Leather herding them toward one of his advance team.

"Everything ready?" asked Leather of his man.

"Yes, sir. The vehicles have been loaded with all the equipment that was sent last night. We're ready to go when you are."

"Anybody taking an interest?"

"Not last night, but they are now." His man indicated a collection of locals staring at them. "I highly recommend we get out of sight."

Leather agreed. "Everyone in the vehicles, quickly."

Laura climbed in the back of one of the three vehicles waiting for them, Leather getting in the front. "Trouble?"

"Not yet. But the sooner we put some distance between ourselves and anyone who saw us arrive on a private charter, the better. This is kidnap and ransom territory."

Acton frowned. "Do we have time for the hotel? Maybe we should just head out."

Leather shook his head as the vehicle pulled away. "No, let's go to the hotel, get everyone inside and out of sight. That will give my men time to keep an eye out for anything suspicious. I'd like to be underway quickly, though. The sooner we're out of here, the better."

Laura nodded. "Agreed. Let's all just freshen up, change our clothes for the road, then head out. One hour?"

"I'll let the others know."

En Route to Site

Mindanao, The Philippines

Acton held on to the Oh Jesus bar as they bounced over yet another pothole. "Lovely roads you've got here, Buwan."

Bautista turned back from the passenger seat, grinning. "You haven't seen anything yet, my friend. Just wait until we start taking the unpaved roads."

Acton chuckled. "Can't wait." He turned back to check on Tommy and Mai sitting in the third row. "How are you two holding up?"

Mai peeled her face away from the window, her eyes as wide as her smile. "It's exciting! It's like a real-life treasure hunt!"

He turned to Tommy who had his face buried in a tablet. "Why don't you look up from that thing once and a while and take in the sights?"

Tommy held up a finger. "Just checking my email."

"You've got a signal?"

"Yup. I'm using Mr. Leather's satphone."

"You can do that?"

Tommy raised his chin long enough to give Acton a look.

Acton held up his hands. "I know, I know, you can do anything when it comes to computers."

Mai wrapped her arms around her boyfriend. "He's my genius."

Tommy blushed then turned off the tablet, unhooking the satphone. "All good on the home front, and we now know we have access if we need it."

Acton took the phone and handed it back up to Leather.

"Better charge that thing, I noticed it was getting low," said Tommy.

Leather handed the phone to Bautista who plugged it into the charger as Leather's radio squawked. "Charlie-One, Charlie-Three, come in, over."

Leather grabbed the radio off the dash, frowning at the voice of his man in the trailing vehicle. "Go ahead, Charlie-Three."

"We've got someone following us."

"You sure?"

"Yeah, I've slowed down and sped up a few times. They're definitely hanging back, looking to see where we're going."

Laura leaned forward. "What are we going to do?"

"What we planned." He slowed the vehicle to a stop and opened the door. "Professor Acton, you're driving. Quickly."

Acton climbed out then into the driver's seat as Leather grabbed a bag off the top of the vehicle. "Where—"

"Just go! Now!"

Leather slammed the door shut and Acton gunned the engine, sending them after the lead vehicle as he watched Leather disappear into the woods, pulling something from the bag.

"I hope he knows what he's doing," said Laura, twisting around to see her head of security.

"If there's anything we can be sure of, it's that."

Leather took cover along the side of the road, the trees and brush thick on either side. He pulled the clear plastic spike strip from his bag, careful not to touch the sharp barbs after unpacking it. He had planned for this. Whoever it was might just be curious, and unless fired upon, he had no intention of killing anyone, yet he couldn't take any chances.

Their pursuers must be stopped.

He could hear the trailing vehicle approaching now, the bend in the road chosen intentionally. It passed and he threw out the strip, the nearly invisible device unfurling across the width of the road. He squawked his comm three times, signaling the trailing vehicle to stop farther on ahead, then receded into the bushes, out of sight, as the suspect vehicle approached.

And smiled as four tires popped, sending the driver into a panic as he struggled to bring the vehicle under control before skidding to a halt farther down the road. Leather yanked on the strip, pulling it out of sight, then quickly rolled it back up, placing it back in his bag before heading deeper into the jungle.

Angry shouts from the occupants of the vehicle helped disguise any noise he might make, and he took advantage of the opportunity to pass their position then catch up to his man stopped ahead. He climbed in and signaled for him to proceed.

"Success?"

Leather nodded. "They won't be bothering us for a while, but there'll be more."

Maliit na Bahay, Mindanao, The Philippines

Laura knelt at the water's edge, the gentle current of the river providing the comfort she needed as she wiped tears from her cheeks. Behind her, hidden from travelers on the river by thick, tall grasses, was the village exactly as expected.

It hadn't been a surprise to find it—the satellite photos had already revealed the jungle's secret on their kitchen counter.

Though seeing it, touching it, was an entirely different experience.

It made it real.

She had read the stories written by the sole survivor, of his happy years as a child, and of that fateful, horrifying day the Japanese had arrived.

Her tears flowed anew as she pictured what it must have been like to go through such a thing, then to have failed to save them.

The guilt must have been overwhelming.

Someone pushed through the grass and she glanced back to find James wiping his own tears away. He sat beside her and she leaned against him, his presence always comforting.

"Part of me was wishing we were wrong."

She looked up at him. "What do you mean?"

He sighed. "If the village wasn't here, then maybe the stories weren't true. Maybe there never was a village."

Her head slowly bobbed as she stared at the river Juan must have escaped on. If only the people who had found him had known what river he came out of, history might have been rewritten, and behind them there might have been a thriving village with Juan's children and grandchildren carrying on his legacy.

Yet there was nothing but silence.

James rose and extended a hand. "Cameron is anxious to get moving. He's concerned we may have more visitors."

She took his hand and rose, then slowly followed him back into the overgrown remains of the village.

Bautista waved at them. "It's an odd name."

"What do you mean?"

"Maliit na Bahay. It literally means Small House."

Laura shrugged. "Sorry, I'm not familiar with Filipino customs when it comes to naming things. Are you saying you don't think that's the name of the place?"

"I wonder. It sounds more to me like what a young child would call their home, as opposed to their village."

James' mouth opened slightly. "That actually makes sense. A lot of isolated villages like this would have very little interaction with those outside of it. Among the children, there wouldn't really be any need to know what the village was actually called. The boy may have just told them what he called his own home."

Laura pointed at the outline of a small building to their left. "For all we know, this could have been Juan's home."

They all paused for a moment, taking in the remains that surrounded them, and the significance they represented. If this was indeed Juan's village, then it meant nearby was a tomb that contained every person he had ever known.

Laura stared up at the hill nearby, the rockface promising. "What we're looking for must be up there." She gathered herself, preparing to focus on the task at hand. "Shall we?"

Bautista hopped up and down. "Please! You have no idea how excited I am right now. This is almost fifteen years of my life's work about to be fulfilled."

Two of Leather's men took point, swinging machetes at the thick underbrush and blazing a path for the rest of them. They formed a line behind the men with Leather taking up the rear. Laura glanced behind her. "Should we leave someone to guard the vehicles?"

Leather shook his head. "We're well out of sight of the road and our recon showed no evidence anyone has been here in years."

Laura's concern eased, as she trusted Leather implicitly. After some incidents on her dig sites in the past, she had sought out the best, and Leather's company's name kept coming up. After several meetings, she had hired his firm to provide security for her projects, and eventually, for James' when they had begun dating. They were expensive, but she was happy to pay it. It gave her peace of mind knowing her students and loved ones were as safe as possible, and she also took pride in the fact everyone employed was a veteran.

Like Leather.

Like her husband, though James would be the first to dispel anyone of the thought he was someone who had seen combat.

Though they both had seen enough over the past several years to fill more than a few novels.

Their close calls with death had prompted her to ask Leather to train her and James in self-defense techniques, along with any students who were interested. This eventually expanded to weapons and tactics, as well as survival skills. And with their skills too often put to the test, she now had a level of self-confidence she could never have imagined before James had entered her life.

He is a bit of a magnet for trouble, isn't he?

Yet she loved him so much it hurt sometimes. She couldn't imagine life without him, and she couldn't imagine their lives being anything other than what they were. Absolutely, life would be safer staying at their jobs and leading a simple life. But why live a life of boredom when there was a world of thrilling discoveries still out there, waiting to be found. Yes, too often that came with danger and heartbreak, yet at the end of the day, new knowledge was revealed, and often the evil among us were brought to justice.

And new friends made along the way.

She glanced at Mai, a perfect example of that.

They emerged into a rough clearing, the rockface revealed. From this new vantage point, she could see that the hill was much more, extending into the distance, increasing significantly in elevation as it did so.

"Look!"

She turned to see where James was pointing and gasped at the sight. A large pile of rubble sat at the base of the hillside just to their left. Exactly as Juan had described.

They rushed toward what might be the collapsed entrance of the cave they had been searching for, as Leather and his men set up a perimeter. Tommy was the first to reach the rocks, and had already scaled the pile before she reached him.

"There's a hole here!" He reached back toward Mai. "Give me the selfie stick."

She pulled it off her hip and handed it up to him. He attached his phone then activated the video function along with the flash. He extended the telescoping pole as far as it would go, counted to five, then pulled it back out. Climbing back down the rocks, everyone gathered around to see what he had recorded.

And gasped collectively as hearts broke.

Narusawa, Japan
July 23rd, 1946

Kijima had never made it home, at least not until many months after the war had ended. They had never made the coast and the awaiting submarine. They had encountered an American patrol, and after a fierce firefight, he and his remaining men had surrendered. It had been almost a year since then, imprisoned in a POW camp on Luzon, isolated from the world, their only news provided by their captors, captors he hadn't believed when they said the war was over.

It was too soon.

How could the Americans have invaded his homeland and beaten its citizenry into submission in mere weeks?

It was impossible.

Then he had learned of the horrible new weapon the Americans possessed. The atomic bomb. Hiroshima and Nagasaki were no more. A single weapon devastating Hiroshima in moments. It was unfathomable. It was the power of the gods unleashed by man.

And when they were shown a newsreel of the aftermath, he had wept with his countrymen, even the Americans in the room disturbed by what they saw. This was a power that should never have been used once, let alone twice, yet as one of the Americans had observed, the nearly 200,000 that had perished had saved many millions more by allowing what would have been the most vicious campaign of World War II to be avoided.

The war was over.

And he was happy.

Yet he still held his secret.

A secret he had no one to tell. The Imperial Army was no more, the command structure was gone, the government was new and a puppet of the American devil MacArthur, and there was no way a mere plebe like him could get near the Emperor to tell him the secret.

And Yamashita was dead, executed by the Americans after his trial in Manila.

He alone knew the secret.

He spotted his home ahead, his village small enough to have escaped much of the destruction he had witnessed in Tokyo. His heart raced as he pushed toward the humble home, every muscle in his body aching from his long journey.

Yet the sight of his wife stepping outside in the midday sun gave him renewed vigor, and he raised his hand, hailing her. "Sakura!"

She turned, her jaw dropping, and the load of laundry she held tumbled from her arms as she ran toward him. He grabbed her in his arms and held her tight, relief sweeping over him as he spotted his son sprinting toward them.

His family had survived.

Intact.

And perhaps it was time to forget the old ways. To forget war.

And to forget the treasure buried in the Philippines, a treasure that should never be allowed to finance another fruitless atrocity.

Maliit na Bahay, Mindanao, The Philippines
Present Day

As Acton worked the jackhammer, he couldn't rid himself of the images of what was on the other side of the rocks he was breaking apart. They had been at it for hours, he, Bautista, and Tommy taking turns at the backbreaking work, and the hole was almost wide enough for a person to get through.

And then they would attempt to explore without desecrating what they had seen. Scores of bodies, skeletal remains, scattered about the cave entrance, too many sitting in place, propped against the stone walls that had become their tomb, some holding each other.

His eyes burned as he wondered which of the remains belonged to Juan's parents, their last breaths taken hoping their son had survived, yet likely certain he hadn't as no one had returned to help them.

They probably thought he had been captured and killed.

He glanced over at Tommy and Mai, and was surprised at the pit in his stomach that burned with rage at the thought of anyone hurting them. Laura had been shot in the stomach several years ago, removing any chance of children in their future, and with their busy and dangerous lives, they had decided against adoption. Instead, they focused all their energies on their students, helping those who came from cash-strapped homes so that they too could take advantage of the opportunities usually only afforded the well off.

Laura and his students were his family, and his life was full. Would he have loved to have had a child of his own to bounce on his knee? Of course, and there were times he cursed the bastard responsible for Laura's injury.

Yet those were private moments. He would never let her know how disappointed he was, for she would take it personally, and never forgive herself for something in no way her fault. He loved her with every fiber of his being, and whether she could bear children affected that love in no way whatsoever.

With their fabulous wealth, they donated to charities that helped the poor, helped children, helped the Third World. They tried to make a difference in the lives of others, and always did it anonymously. They weren't out to be known as philanthropists—they were content to stay out of the limelight.

He didn't begrudge those who sought it, as long as in the end they were doing good. If getting on camera was what it took for some millionaire or Hollywood type to part with their cash, then so be it.

It wasn't for him, and it wasn't for Laura.

The stone he was working on finally split then tumbled away, and he stepped back, turning off the jackhammer. "I think we're through."

He handed the tool down to Tommy who placed it out of the way. Acton cleared some loose debris then held out a hand. "Flashlight, please."

Someone slapped one in his hand and he flicked it on, shining it into the hole they had created. He climbed through with ease, coming out on the other side. He shone the light around, making sure the roof wasn't about to cave in on them with the slightest step.

"I think it's safe. Everybody watch your step when you come through. There are remains everywhere."

Bautista was the next through. Acton helped him inside then pulled through a battery-operated lamp they had brought, handing it over to Bautista who went to work unfolding it then turning it on. Acton helped Laura through, and she gasped at the now lit chamber. He took a quick look and a lump formed in his throat, the video Tommy had taken not doing the find justice. Mai and Tommy were through next then Acton poked his head out to find Leather.

"You guys coming in?"

Leather shook his head. "We'll keep an eye out. If anything happens, turn out the lights in there and keep quiet. I'm going to go for a quick recon, just in case our friends have decided to try again."

Acton frowned. "Okay, keep safe."

"You too, Professor." Leather paused. "And Professor?"

"Yes?"

"Try not to take too long."

Acton laughed. "Have we met?" He crawled back inside to find the others all standing, taking in the sight of the scores upon scores of bodies.

"I think there can be little doubt these are the villagers Juan spoke of," said Bautista.

Acton agreed. "We'll document all of this when we have time. For now, let's head deeper in and see if what we think is here actually is. Nobody will kill us because we found bodies, but they will if they think we've found gold." He held out his hand. "Buwan, why don't you lead the way. This is your discovery."

Bautista smiled. "This is *our* discovery. There is no way I'd be here without you and your wife."

Acton shrugged. "Have it your way. We keep the gold."

Bautista laughed, the sound echoing off the walls, and he abruptly stopped as he remembered they were inside an involuntary crypt. He inched forward, past the bodies gathered near the cave entrance, and they soon thinned. Acton was keeping a mental tally, having given up counting the sets of bones, as too many were piled on each other, the sight of what were clearly mothers, fathers, and children huddled together in their final moments overwhelming. Instead, he began counting sets of clothing, and had lost count past two hundred when they arrived in a large chamber, hollowed out over millennia by what was likely an underground river at some point.

And his jaw dropped.

Scores of crates, many broken open, filled the area. Gold and silver, precious jewels and more, glinted in the beams of their flashlights.

Bautista was spinning in the center of the chamber, his arms outstretched as he laughed, a life's work finally realized.

And Acton was happy for him, his own smile wide as he hugged an equally excited Laura.

Yamashita's Gold.

The legend was true. The size of the find epic. There were hundreds of crates, if not over a thousand. It would take weeks if not months to properly catalog, and that would be only the beginning.

For who did it belong to?

After all, it was all stolen. Yet so much had been melted down into gold bars, who was to say who the original owner was?

And there was definitely billions here. Tens of billions at least. It was enough to change a lot of lives for the better.

Enough to kill for.

He drew a long breath and exhaled loudly.

Laura looked up at him. "What?"

"This is too big."

"What do you mean?"

"I mean, if anyone catches wind of this, they won't hesitate to kill us all."

Leather cursed at the sight ahead. Their tail now had two friends and a new truck with four perfectly good tires. They were stopped for a piss break not half a klick from where the lost village was, as well as a bunch of civilians who had no idea how to be quiet.

He activated his comm. "This is Charlie-One. Go dark, I repeat, go dark, out."

He could take out all four hostiles with little trouble, however he couldn't justify it yet. They were all armed, definitely on the wrong side of good, but hadn't done anything yet to merit their deaths. He couldn't be certain they were after his people, nor could he be certain they'd even find them if they were. If everyone kept quiet and out of sight, these guys might just drive past the village.

He stared at the road and cursed, their tire tracks clearly visible, along with others that had traveled on the roads since the last rains. When they had reached the area, they had bushwhacked a trail to the village, then driven in once they had confirmed its location.

Their departure from the road was obvious.

He had to cover their tracks.

He carefully made his way farther down the road, and once out of the unwelcome visitors' line of sight, he sprinted to their exit point.

An exit point so painfully obvious, there was no way these guys would miss it. He grabbed a few limbs of the trees cut down earlier and gripped them at the stalks, brushing the thick leaves against the dirt, obscuring the tire tracks leading off the road. Satisfied it was no longer obvious, he hacked at several bushes away from the road and hauled them into place, doing his best to make the moved shrubbery appear natural.

The roar of an engine and grinding of gears had him falling back into the forest and taking cover. He watched as the truck slowly drove by, all four men examining the tree line, none watching the road, all missing the fact their tire tracks had stopped.

And none spotting his handiwork with the shrubbery.

He waited until they were out of sight, then sprinted back toward the cave.

For they weren't out of the woods yet.

All it would take would be for just one of those four to notice the tire tracks created by three heavy vehicles were no longer in front of them.

Then they'd be back.

He arrived in the clearing to find his men holding their positions, the cave silent.

"What did you see?" asked one of his men.

"Our tail was back with a couple of friends. I obscured our exit point, but if they've got half a brain between them, they'll figure it out eventually." He pointed at him. "Get down to the road and keep an eye out. Radio if you see anything, but don't engage. Fall back if there's trouble."

"Yes, sir." His man jogged down the cleared path and Leather went to the freshly opened hole. "Professors, I need to speak with you!" he called, his voice echoing inside.

"Coming!" replied Laura, and within minutes she and Acton were outside, the others climbing through as well. He didn't wait for them.

"We've got a problem."

Laura's eyes narrowed. "What?"

"Our tail was back. Bigger truck, four guns this time. They were stopped at the road having a break. I took the opportunity to deal with the disturbance in the brush we made when we left the road, and it fooled them for the moment, but they'll be back. My guess is if they're looking for us, then they have another vehicle coming from the opposite direction. When they meet up without having found us, they'll come back, checking out everything with a fine-toothed comb."

Acton frowned as he put an arm around Laura's shoulders. "Any idea who they are?"

"Probably Islamic fundamentalists. The place is crawling with them. Likely MILF"—he glanced at Tommy who held his tongue, fear instead on his face as he held Mai—"but it doesn't matter. Whoever they are, they're trouble, and not out for a Sunday drive. They know we're out here and will be searching the area soon."

"What do we do?" asked Laura.

"It's too late to head back. We wouldn't even get halfway before it was dark, and they might have a roadblock set up. I'm going to call in my backup team. They'll be in Cotabato City by morning, and they can head this way, making sure there are no roadblocks. If they encounter anything, they'll just turn back."

"Won't that look suspicious?"

Leather shook his head. "No, they'll have a drone on point. They'll see anything long before they reach it."

"I wish we had a drone," muttered Tommy.

"We did, but it was confiscated when we arrived. Local regulations. We weren't able to acquire a new one locally in time that was compatible with our systems. There are no cellular networks out here, and Bluetooth just doesn't cut it in the jungle."

Laura sucked in a deep breath, then exhaled slowly as she regarded everyone he knew she felt responsible for. "And you're sure they're after us?"

"Not one hundred percent. I doubt they know who we are, otherwise they'd be putting more of an effort into it. My guess is that they know white people arrived on a charter plane and left with private security. They likely have people watching the airport for potential victims. This is how these people make their money. They take tourists hostage, hold them for ransom, and too often it's paid." He jabbed a finger at the cave. "And if they find this, they won't care about any ransom. They'll kill you in a heartbeat. This funds a thousand years of Jihad against the West."

"Can we call for help?" asked Mai. "The police?"

"None that we can trust. The backup team is our best bet, however, umm"—he turned to Laura—"I was thinking we might need a little, ahh, Kraft Dinner type of help."

Bautista's eyes narrowed. "Kraft Dinner. What is that?"

Acton smiled. "A tasty cheap meal."

Laura chuckled. "And a good friend."

"I'll send the message, but there's no guarantee he'll get it in time."

Leather shrugged. "It might be our only—"

Tommy pointed at the sky. "Speaking of drones, there's one now. Could your guys already be here?"

Leather looked up at where Tommy was pointing and shook his head. "No. I haven't even called them yet."

"The terrorists?" asked Laura, fear tinging her voice.

"I don't think so. That looks military to me."

Philippine Army National Headquarters
Fort Bonifacio, Manila, The Philippines

"We've got people at the site."

Colonel Ocampo looked up from his phone then rounded his cousin's desk to see the live feed from the drone General Cruz had dispatched earlier by a rapid reaction force he had inserted into the area. The laptop showed a group of people and equipment near the side of a cliff with a pile of rocks in front of it. "Is it the Yakuza?"

Cruz tapped each face on the screen, the computer pulling images of the targets and displaying them. He pointed at a female. "She looks Asian, though I don't think she's Japanese. These four are Americanos." He indicated another. "He's definitely one of us. And so are these three with guns."

"Private security?"

"Likely. They look professional."

"Show the video again."

His cousin complied.

Ocampo leaned in. "There's a lot of equipment there. I think that's a jackhammer. That means they definitely know about the gold."

"But if they're not the Yakuza, then who the hell are they?"

"And how did they find out?"

Cruz leaned back in his chair and folded his arms. "The bigger question is what do we do?"

"Kill them?"

Cruz shook his head. "Not before we know who they are." He pursed his lips, tapping his chin. "Or maybe..."

"What?"

He glared at Ocampo. "Will you let me think, dammit!"

Ocampo retreated to the other side of the desk. If these people were at the site, and they had equipment for breaking through the rocks blocking the entrance, then it could only mean one thing.

He hopped up and down, the excitement too much to contain.

"Will you stop that! Why are you so happy? This is a serious problem!"

Ocampo stopped, but the smile remained. "Don't you realize what this means?"

"What?"

"It means the map is accurate."

Cruz's eyes narrowed. "What makes you so sure?"

"Because exactly where that X is on the map, we find a group of people with equipment, at the side of a mountain with a pile of rocks. It matches everything I was told by that Takashi kid. The gold *has* to be there." He reached over the desk and grabbed his cousin's shoulder. "Cousin, we're going to be rich! So rich, we'll be able to buy our own island! We'll be able to buy Hawaii!"

Cruz batted Ocampo's hand away. "Yeah, but first we need to get rid of *that* problem, then deal with the local problem."

Ocampo shook his head. "It doesn't matter. We can do whatever we need to do, then just pay off whoever needs to be paid off to get away with it. Don't you get it? We're talking hundreds of billions of dollars. That's trillions of pesos. Even if we had to give a million pesos to a million people, we'd still have more than enough."

Cruz grunted. "I think your math is a little off, but I see your point. We have to stop thinking in terms that real people think in." He smiled. "I think I'm beginning to understand how men like Marcos and Estrada thought. They had so much money, the laws simply didn't apply to them."

"And they no longer apply to us. We can kill dozens. Hundreds! And no one will care when we just hand them a single gold bar out of our thousands. But we have to act fast. If these people are already there, who knows who else is on their way?"

Cruz frowned. "Eventually all the money in the world won't be able to buy the silence we need for a massacre that size." He stared at the images of the trespassers, especially the Americanos. "We can't just kill these people. They could be American. European. It will pose too many questions."

"Then what do we do?"

"We need to get them out of there long enough for us to secure the site, but do it so MILF doesn't get suspicious." His eyes widened. "I think I have an idea of how we could kill two birds with one stone." A smile spread. "I think I have an excellent idea."

Cotabato Airport

Cotabato, Mindanao, The Philippines

Hiroki yanked at his shirt as he descended the stairs and walked toward the terminal of the small airport. All was supposed to have been arranged through Akira. His only orders were to meet with the local contact who would act as their driver and guide, and find the damned gold.

And it was a race against time.

Apparently, Takashi had arrived in Tokyo, and before Akira's people could intercept him, a contact sent by the Filipinos had reached him first.

The map was in their hands now.

And this was their country, so they had to act fast. If they found the gold, they were to let Akira know so he could arrange transport and more men, then the idea was to get as much of it out of the cave and hidden elsewhere until they could get it back to Japan.

Even a small fraction of it could be worth hundreds of millions of yen, though it would be worthless if the Filipino authorities caught them in the act.

How much they retrieved, he didn't care. In fact, he was hoping there was nothing there, because then failure wouldn't be his fault. Takashi and his great-grandfather would be the ones to pay the price for lying to the oyabun.

But if the gold was there, and he were to fail in retrieving it, *he'd* be the one paying the price.

He rubbed the tip of his pinky finger, the portion up to the knuckle removed for showing disrespect to the oyabun when intoxicated years ago.

It was a valuable lesson learned, and he rarely drank now as he knew he had a loose tongue.

And as he had discovered, it was indeed harder to grip his sword, though that mattered little in this day. The tradition was ancient, and forced the weakened member of the organization to rely more heavily on the others. The dishonor, and its punishment, taught the offender that the brotherhood was everything, and they were all dependent upon each other, especially the weakened ones. And with each punishment, another portion of a digit was removed, making the person's grip on his sword ever weaker.

And the reliance on his brothers ever greater.

Today, he'd just use a gun, though the point had been made.

He climbed into the passenger seat of the vehicle their guide had arranged. They were four plus the guide with lots of room in the back to pile gold should they find it.

"Are you sure you want to head out now? It's very late. The sun will be setting soon."

Hiroki motioned ahead. "Yes. There's no time to waste."

Their guide shrugged. "Your choice." He aimed a thumb over his shoulder at the third row. "You better gear up. This could get ugly."

Maliit na Bahay, Mindanao, The Philippines

Acton warmed his hands near the flames of their small fire built near the forest's edge to reduce the likelihood of it being seen. It was now dark, the stars and a half-moon providing the only light besides the fire, flashlight and screens kept to a minimum.

Leather returned from the clearing and its open skies so necessary for the satphone, then took his position in the circle around the flame. "I managed to arrange a helicopter evac for tomorrow morning. The pilot says he can leave at sunrise, but will wait to hear from me, just in case we find another way out."

Laura poked at the fire with a stick. "Is that likely?"

"No. He's just reluctant to come out here."

Tommy grunted. "He's probably thinking we'll be dead by then. It'll save him a trip."

Mai swatted him. "Quit being so negative."

He shrugged. "Sorry. But don't be expecting an upbeat podcast when we get back."

Acton's eyebrows rose. "Podcast?"

Mai beamed. "He's been podcasting for a while now. He's really funny. Has guests on and everything. He has tens of thousands of followers."

Tommy smiled shyly. "Actually, I crossed a hundred thousand a few weeks back."

"What's it about?" asked Laura.

"Life as a millennial in a post-boomer/Gen Xer world."

Acton eyed him. "So, bitching and moaning about how life isn't fair?"

"Haw-haw. Nooo, more about how we have so many technologies that could make life easier and better, that could solve so many of today's problems, yet because we aren't in charge yet, these solutions are ignored."

Acton was intrigued. "Such as?"

"Well, you know how you hate social media?"

"I know very well."

"Well, why is that?"

"There's a myriad of reasons, but one is that anonymity has allowed hate to flourish. There's no room for respectful discourse anymore."

"Exactly. And what if I told you there was a solution to that problem, but it would take some balls to implement it."

Acton's eyebrows shot up. "Okay, you've got my attention."

"There's a group working on a blockchain solution to Internet access. You would create an account on this system that links back to you personally. You can only do it once, and no one else can pretend to be you. That way, anything you post on the Internet while logged in through this blockchain, will be linked back specifically to you."

"Sounds draconian."

Tommy waved a hand to dismiss the criticism. "Don't get me wrong. You can still go on the Internet and browse whatever you want, download whatever. That's not the idea here. You can even go on sites that don't want to use it. The point is that the reputable companies will want to implement this login feature. Take Facebook, for example. If every account were verified, then every fake news story, every hate crime, every bullying post, would link back to a specific person. If somebody posts something libelous, then the victim can sue, the court can order Facebook to identify the person, and bingo! You've got a name and address. No more fake accounts from the Russians or Chinese. All these problems are taken care of."

Laura's head bobbed. "So basically, because everyone will know exactly who you are, you won't post the hateful garbage we see all the time, and instead might tone it down?"

"Exactly."

Acton pursed his lips. "It sounds like a great idea. Disagreement is fine. Our country has always gotten along in the modern age, even with splits along party lines. But over the past decade or so, especially now, things are so vicious, we're heading into trouble. This 'if you're not on my side you're evil' way of thinking has to stop otherwise this country risks failing."

Laura tossed her stick into the fire. "But won't people just leave Facebook and go somewhere else?"

Tommy nodded. "They could, but remember, more and more regulations are being implemented worldwide to make these platforms accountable for their content. Anything that gains traction will be forced to implement a solution, and the blockchain might be the easiest and quickest. Eventually, if you want to spew your hate and vitriol, you'll be on the Dark Web instead of on the Internet where 99% of us live."

Acton smiled. "I think I might have to start listening to your podcast. This Gen Xer needs a dose of schooling."

Laura bumped his shoulder with hers. "Don't try to sound cool, dear, it rarely works."

Acton faked a pout. "That really hurts. Don't you know it's hip to be square?"

"Now, that reference is so old, I might just think you're a Boomer."

He grinned at her. "So, you're into old men, are you?"

She patted his leg. "You're old enough for me." She turned to Tommy. "Do you find it difficult to talk to that many people?"

He shrugged. "At first, I don't think I could have done it, but when I started, I think Mai was my only listener. I slowly built a fanbase, and with each new podcast I got a little better. Now, I don't even think about it. Put me behind my microphone and I'll talk to a hundred thousand people without breaking a sweat. Put me in front of a room with a dozen people, and I'm soaked in flop sweat."

Acton chuckled. "Reminds me of my first class. I was sweating buckets. Luckily, there *were* literally twelve people there. If the class was packed like it is now, I think I would have fainted."

Laura leaned her head on his shoulder. "Aww, the price of fame."

"Yup. The Kardashians have nothing on me."

Tommy laughed. "Keepin' up with the Actons!"

Laura rolled her eyes. "Can you imagine?"

Bautista sprung to his feet and began pacing. Acton looked up at him. "What's wrong?"

"I'm sorry, Jim, but, well, we're talking about leaving here in the morning."

"So?"

"So? What about the gold?"

"We'll have to worry about that later. Our lives are more important."

Bautista vehemently shook his head, slicing at the air with his hand. "No. This is my life's work. I won't leave it."

Acton smiled gently at the man, understanding his angst. Both he and Laura over the years had been irrational at times when it came to protecting valuable or significant finds in the face of danger, and sometimes it had cost them dearly.

And now, on the opposite side of the equation, he understood how he must have looked to people like their friends Reading and Dawson.

Irrational.

"Buwan, nobody knows why we're here, which means nobody knows about the find. We'll leave tomorrow morning then come back when we've thought this through better. Maybe more security, a larger group with government involvement. Something too big for a few bad guys to interfere with."

Bautista shook his head. "They'll just steal it. It's happened before." He jabbed a finger toward the cave. "This is too important to just let the government deal with it. They'll take it all, hand it out to their buddies, and the public will never know about it." He shook his head. "Don't you understand? All those people died to protect this secret. We owe it to them to make sure the world knows about their sacrifice, their murders. If we let the government deal with this, we risk their secret never being revealed."

Acton felt for the man. He truly did. His concern wasn't the gold either, it was the people. The cave behind him was a tomb that deserved to be treated with respect, and Bautista was right to be worried about involving the government. Unfortunately, the Philippines was notoriously corrupt, having a score of only 36 out of 100 on the Corruption Perception Index. It was a definite possibility that the find could be hidden from the public and the valuables inside pilfered by the corrupt.

Yet preventing that possible eventuality wasn't worth their lives.

"I'm afraid, Buwan, that we don't have a choice. We have to leave first thing in the morning."

Bautista dropped back into his spot around the fire. "I know, I know. It's just so frustrating to be so close, and to lose it all because of gangs of thieves who pretend to be fundamentalists."

Acton reached over and squeezed his friend's shoulder. "We'll figure it out, buddy. Like I've always said, things always have a way of working out."

Laura nodded. "Sometimes in ways you least expect."

Approaching Maliit na Bahay, Mindanao, The Philippines

Their driver pointed at the road ahead, now bathed in darkness, the sun having set only minutes before, their headlights barely slicing a path.

"We should stop. It's too dangerous."

Hiroki shook his head, staring at the GPS. "No, we're almost there."

"But this place is crawling with MILF. We're sitting ducks."

"Keep driving. We'll deal with—"

Lights suddenly turned on ahead and their driver slammed on the brakes. Silhouettes of men carrying what were likely AK-47s were highlighted by the high-beams of the vehicle blocking their path, and Hiroki cursed as he realized their driver had been right.

"Turn out the lights."

"What?"

"Do what I say."

The driver turned out the lights and Hiroki grabbed the bag at his feet filled with his gear, then gripped his door handle. "Everybody out and into the trees. Now!" He shoved his door open and sprinted for cover, hitting the ground as gunfire erupted. He rolled to a knee, taking up position behind a tree, then drew his pistol, emptying the mag into the front of the vehicle, killing the lights, the entire scene now shrouded in darkness.

He unzipped his bag and pulled out the night-vision goggles inside, fitting them over his head. He flipped down the goggles and assessed the situation as he reloaded. Their driver was dead behind the wheel, but no one else appeared to be in the vehicle.

His men had followed his orders without hesitation.

Like loyal Yakuza should.

"Open fire!" he ordered as he took aim, squeezing the trigger at the targets highlighted in his goggles. The enemy were scrambling for cover, but several were already down. He counted at least six still moving, and let the others keep them ducking while he picked them off when they came up to fire.

Unfortunately, he wasn't a great shot.

Gunplay wasn't very common in Japan, his expertise mostly acquired while playing Ghost Recon.

A thunderous entrant to the field of battle changed everything, a bright muzzle flash overwhelming his goggles, forcing him to look away, though not before spotting the source.

A mounted weapon in the rear of the vehicle, likely a .50 cal or equivalent.

He heard a cry to his left, one of his comrades going down, then another. He took aim and emptied his pistol toward the raging weapon, squeezing the trigger repeatedly until he was out, one of his last shots finding its mark.

The weapon fell silent.

He took the opportunity to advance through the trees as he reloaded. The remaining terrorists—for that's whom he assumed they were—scrambled to re-man the silent weapon. A single position on his side still fired, and he realized there were only two of them left against what still appeared to be four.

Yet he didn't fire, instead continuing to advance as silently as he could, his goggles giving him the best view of the battlefield of anyone on it.

And within moments, he was behind them.

He emerged from the trees, all four targets visible, hiding behind the vehicle as they fired toward his last surviving comrade.

He started from the left.

And then there was silence.

"Is anyone still alive?"

Koji replied. "I am. You?"

He chuckled. "I think so. Check on the others. I'm going to make sure these guys are dead." He made the rounds, putting a bullet in each of the two wounded, then climbed into the vehicle and tried to start the engine.

No joy.

He put it in neutral and pushed it to the side of the road, then was joined by Koji who helped drag the bodies out of the way.

"The others?"

"Dead. That fifty got them."

Hiroki frowned. "We'll leave them for now. More could be on the way."

"Are we heading back?"

Hiroki regarded his friend. "What do you think Akira would want?"

Koji grunted. "For us to have died with the others."

"You're probably right. Let's keep going and report in. He'll want to know about what just happened."

Maliit na Bahay, Mindanao, The Philippines

Acton had a protective arm around Laura as they all stood, staring in the direction of the heavy gunfire exchanged in the distance, a distance that sounded far too close.

"Sounds like it's only a couple of klicks away," observed Leather, a handgun supplied by one of his men at the ready.

A large weapon opened up for almost a minute then fell silent, the gunfire dwindling, then abruptly stopping, leaving an eerie calm before the wildlife once again resumed their constant din.

"What the hell was that?" asked Tommy. "MILF?"

Leather kicked dirt on the fire, quickly extinguishing it with little smoke to reveal their position. "One side of it, maybe, but there were two sides to that skirmish."

"Police?" suggested Laura.

Mai's eyes were like saucers. "Maybe they can help us?"

Leather shook his head. "No, we don't know who won, and we don't know who was fighting. For all we know, it was two MILF cells fighting each other."

Acton kicked some more dirt on the fire, an ember having flared. "What's your recommendation?"

"Get some sleep. We'll keep watch, then first thing in the morning I'll call for the chopper."

"Won't they hear it?"

"Let's hope they've moved on by then, or if they do, we're long gone before they reach us." Leather regarded the group. "And that's critically important. When that chopper arrives, there isn't a second of hesitation from anyone." His eyes rested on Bautista. "We leave everything. We just get on board and we lift off. I don't want that thing on the ground for more than sixty seconds. He lands, we rush the doors and get in. Understood?"

Everyone nodded, including a reluctant Bautista.

Philippine Army National Headquarters
Fort Bonifacio, Manila, The Philippines

"Are you sure this is a good idea?"

Ocampo's heart was racing, the plan proposed by his cousin beyond anything he had considered when he had first walked into his office earlier. Yet in reality, it was fruit from the idea he had planted.

The law no longer applied to them.

Nor, apparently, morality.

With the find all but confirmed, the wealth they were about to possess changed everything, and should a couple of handfuls of people die as a result, who cared?

His cousin certainly didn't, and though his stomach was telling him otherwise, neither did he.

These weren't his people.

The Americanos were irrelevant, and the Filipinos were traitors as far as he was concerned. The idea of protecting rich white people as they looted his country disgusted him.

They deserved to die.

All of them.

They were taking what belonged to the Filipino people, and yes, the irony was not lost on him that he was attempting to do the same. Yet he was Filipino, and his family and friends would benefit, and indirectly his country.

His cousin finally looked up from the secure laptop he was using to direct the covert operation initiated hours before. "What did you say?"

"I asked you if you were sure this was a good idea."

"I am."

"But what if they find out?"

"Who?"

"Any number of people. The President comes to mind."

"He won't. You and I are the only ones who know what is going on here. And besides, there's no time. Your own contact said a group of Japanese businessmen arrived at the Cotabato Airport a few hours ago. That has to be the Yakuza. They'll be at the site in the morning, and they'll be armed. They'll take out these people before we have a chance to act, then the entire plan will fail." He shook his head. "No, there's no choice. We have to act now if we have any chance of succeeding."

The Lotus

Tokyo, Japan

"It's only me and Koji left. We managed to eliminate them all, but there'll be more coming to look for them when they don't report in."

Takashi listened through a haze of pain to Hiroki's update from the Philippines with dread, a displeased Akira having put it on speaker. And his captor's rage was building with each word.

Akira shoved the woman in his lap to the floor and rose, pacing the room, saying nothing.

"What should we do?"

He spun toward the phone. "What should you do? You keep going, that's what you do! We need to know if the gold is real!"

"But if more arrive, there are only two of us left, and we're low on ammo. We never expected a firefight. Not like that."

Akira sat back down, bending over to be closer to the phone sitting on the table, intent on making sure his rage was heard at the other end.

"I don't care. Confirm the gold is there, call it in, then get back to safety if you can. Knowing whether the gold is there or not is more important than your lives, understood?"

A subdued Hiroki replied. "Yes, sir."

Akira ended the call and stared at Takashi. "Two of my men are dead. If your hiijiisan is lying, he's dead too."

Takashi struggled to sit up but failed. "Yet you still sent the rest."

Akira shrugged. "What's a few lives when hundreds of billions are at stake?"

"What about your humanity?"

Akira regarded him for a moment, the anger gone from his reply. "I lost that the moment I was born into this family."

"You could always leave."

Akira grunted, leaning back in his chair. "A man in my position never leaves the Yakuza." He downed a shot of sake. "Alive."

Maliit na Bahay, Mindanao, The Philippines

Hiroki crept through the jungle, his night-vision goggles in place, Koji behind him. They had parked on the road, as it was too dangerous to try and push through the jungle in the dark, though it was obvious from what he was now seeing that someone had earlier, the tire tracks evident, their iridescent green tread marks like glowing lane markers leading the way.

They came out into an area where the trees were less mature, a small river to the left, and as he continued forward, his heart leaped as his head slowly pivoted to the right.

Three vehicles were parked in the open.

He dropped to a knee, Koji doing the same, quickly scanning the area for the owners, finding nothing on his goggles. He listened for voices, anything human, yet there was nothing beyond the jungle.

"More terrorists?" asked Koji in a whisper.

Hiroki shook his head. "I don't think so. These are too nice."

"Tourists?"

"Only tourists would be stupid enough to be out here at this time of night."

"We are."

"And you think we're smart?"

Koji chuckled. "Not today."

Hiroki rose, circling the vehicles, and spotted a heavy concentration of boot prints heading in one direction. He pointed. "We've got footprints. Let's follow them."

"And if we find someone?"

"Shoot first, ask questions later."

"Why not, it worked out so well last time."

Park Hyatt Beijing

Beijing, China

"I miss you too, babe. What did you get up to today?"

CIA Special Agent Dylan Kane yanked at his tie, tossing it onto the bed as he held his phone out, the love of his life on the other end, her voice slightly altered in case they were being listened to.

After all, Lee Fang was a wanted fugitive and a traitor as far as the Chinese government was concerned.

"You know me. Worked out, watched some TV. I'm having dinner with Sherrie later. I'm not sure if Chris will be there."

He unbuttoned his shirt, walking over to the window. He stared at the incredible view of the polluted city below. He loved the vibrancy of Beijing, yet ached at how the population was treated, so many indoctrinated to believe it was perfectly fine for the state to monitor every aspect of their lives.

"Say hi for me."

"I will. How was your flight?"

"Not too bad. Business-class can be rough, you know."

She giggled as he paced the perimeter of the room. Unbeknownst to anyone who might be listening in through any eavesdropping devices planted in his room, his phone was scanning for bugs—audio or video—each edge of the phone capable of vibrating independently in varying degrees of frequency, to guide him to any unwanted signals in the room without anyone knowing.

"You should request a private jet next time. I'm sure your company can afford it."

His phone vibrated.

The right side.

He turned, allowing it to guide him toward a light switch. Once close enough, his phone analyzed the transmission emanating from it, and determined it was audio-only.

He did nothing.

"Something tells me they wouldn't approve the paperwork."

"You never know until you ask."

He continued his scan, his phone vibrating again, pulsing rapidly as he reached the center of the room.

Where there was nowhere for a bug to be hidden.

Or is there?

He feigned a stretch, extending his arms into the air, and his phone went nuts as it neared the ceiling fan.

"This is true. I should try it. Shaw's of London is very generous, and I am one of their top insurance investigators."

"You are that."

He glanced at the phone.

Video.

It made sense. The vantage point gave them a complete view of the room.

And it was difficult to casually block.

He finished his sweep, finding nothing else, then pulled his toiletry kit from his suitcase. "I'm going to take a long soak in the bath, okay? I'll call you later."

"Have fun!"

"Not much fun to be had in a tub without you."

She laughed. "Then keep me on the line, I'll talk you through it."

Something twinged. "Don't tempt me. Love you."

"Love you too."

He ended the call then stepped into the bathroom and ran the bath. A quick scan showed another device behind the mirror, though that wasn't his concern. He emptied his toiletries as he tapped away on his phone, pretending to check messages. Instead, he was hijacking the signal transmitted from the devices in his room while he wasn't in it.

He finished undressing, displaying his assets to whoever was watching, then climbed into the bath, turning off the tap. He closed his eyes and was soon asleep.

Or so those watching might think.

He tapped a button on his phone, still gripped in his hand dangling out of sight outside the tub.

It vibrated three times, confirming success.

He climbed out, the transmitter built into his suitcase hijacking all the signals. He'd be secure for a few minutes, long enough to check his encrypted messages. He logged in and quickly scrolled through several from his handler along with some contacts he had made along the way, then paused.

What now?

It was a message from his old professor, James Acton. Acton had a habit of needing help, and with everything he and his wife had done for Kane and his friends over the years, he was happy to oblige.

He just wished Acton had better timing.

He dialed the number left in the message, Acton answering immediately.

"Hey, Doc, it's me. Make it quick, I've only got a few minutes."

"Okay, sorry for troubling you, but we've got a situation and need some advice. We're in the Philippines. I sent you the coordinates in the message. We had some locals follow us, but we think we've lost them for the moment."

"Probably local radicals. That place is notorious for kidnap and ransom."

"Yeah, Cameron tried to warn us."

"Leather is with you?"

"Yes. He has three local hires with him."

"Armed?"

"Yes."

"Anything else suspicious?"

"We just heard a large firefight that lasted a few minutes. Cameron thinks it was about two klicks from here. We don't know who was involved."

"Could be anyone in that area. Don't assume it was anybody friendly."

"We're not."

"What's Cameron's plan?"

"He's arranged a chopper to evac us first thing in the morning."

"That's the safest bet. I'd stay off the roads."

"Yeah, we will. I'm just concerned that whoever is out there could be looking for us. We were kind of conspicuous."

"Let me guess, private jet?"

"Well, we weren't that stupid, but it was a private charter."

Kane chuckled. "Jet or prop, it doesn't matter in that area. It's all about the Benjamins." He became serious. "Listen, I suggest you follow Leather's instructions to the letter. He knows what he's doing."

"I've gathered that."

"And Doc?"

"Yeah?"

"If the shit hits the fan, just surrender."

"What?"

"Surrender. Let them capture you. They'll hold you for ransom. If I don't hear from you in the morning, I'll get you out. I'll come in with a team myself if I have to. The key to surviving this is not getting yourselves killed in a firefight."

"Shit!" hissed Acton.

Kane tensed. "What?"

"I just heard something. It sounded like a twig snapping."

Kane stood in the bath, water rushing down his body. "Give me Leather, now!"

"Just a sec."

There was some static then Leather's voice answered. "Go ahead."

"Leave them."

"What?" Leather clearly didn't like the suggestion.

"Leave them now. Take the phone and track them, then let me know where they take them."

"I can't leave them."

"Do it. Trust me. You know I'm right. A firefight gets them killed."

Leather sighed. "If anything happens to them—"

"Then it was going to happen anyway."

Maliit na Bahay, Mindanao, The Philippines

Leather ended the call, a frown creasing his face as he processed Kane's recommendation. And that was all it was. They weren't orders to follow. Yet the CIA operator was right.

They couldn't win a firefight.

He watched out of the corner of his eye as his men advanced toward the sound they had just heard, their weapons drawn, ready to repel any hostiles.

He turned to his employer. "Kane wants me to leave you alone and track you if things go south."

Laura replied without hesitation. "Do it."

"I can't leave you."

"No, he's right. If no one knows where we are, then we're dead." She put a hand on his shoulder. "Go. Now."

Another cracking sound from the jungle settled the debate. He drew the Glock provided earlier by one of his men, then pocketed the satphone. He turned to the group. "Good luck. I'll come back for you, I promise."

Laura smiled. "I know you will."

He rushed into the jungle, opposite where the sounds of advancing hostiles were coming from, and pressed through the trees, his chest aching, his stomach churning as he was overwhelmed with a sense of having betrayed his clients.

And his friends.

James placed his hands on her shoulders as Laura watched Leather disappear in the darkness, and with him any sense of security she might have felt only moments before.

He was their guardian.

And he was gone.

Knowing the man, he was probably torn by Kane's recommendation, yet her husband's former student was right. They needed to be tracked if this was indeed about to turn into a hostage situation.

Something moved in the shadows and she gasped.

"Everyone down!" hissed James as he extended his arms and forced them all toward the cave entrance and the limited shelter the large stones provided.

One of the security guards started speaking in a loud voice using his native tongue, likely ordering whoever was approaching to identify themselves. The man sounded calm—far calmer than she was—and professional.

Cameron chose well.

James had them against the rockface now, his body draped over hers, Tommy over Mai, and out of the direct line of fire.

A barrage of bullets erupted behind them and Laura twisted to see what was going on. Muzzle flashes lit the jungle as whoever it was engaged the security team. They returned fire as they spread out, splitting the enemy's focus while laying down their own wall of lead. Someone cried out from the tree line, then another, and Laura felt for a moment as if this might go their way, though judging from the number of positions firing, they were outnumbered at least two-to-one.

Another cry, and one of the defensive positions fell dark, then another, leaving one lone soul to defend them all.

Then there was silence, even the jungle mourning the dead.

The trees rustled and their victorious attackers advanced into the clearing. Her ears were pounding as she struggled to control her breathing, to remember her training, and to remember they weren't dead yet.

James brought clarity. "Everybody just stay calm. No threatening moves. You know what they said. We'll be taken hostage if we just remain calm."

Her husband stood, his hands raised high as he turned to face the enemy.

And she whimpered at his words.

"We surrender."

With every fiber of his being, Leather resisted jumping into the fray. His men were dead, but the people he was protecting were not.

And he had clear shots of the half-dozen Islamists that had just executed the attack. If he were lucky, if his aim were true, he could take them all down, perhaps even before they got off a shot.

Yet everything would have to go perfectly, and all it would take would be for one to open fire on Laura and the others for it to go south quickly.

No, he had to resist the urge to intervene. He had to carry out the plan Kane had laid out.

He had to let them be captured.

He watched as the hostages were bound, a blubbering Bautista translating the shouted orders. Thankfully, no one attempted to escape, no one resisted, everyone playing their part.

Be a good hostage.

Let them believe the ransom will be paid.

And trust that he would be true to his word and rescue them.

He swiftly moved through the trees, using the shouts and arrogance of his enemy to provide cover, circling back to where they had come from. He was assuming they had traveled in a vehicle, and he couldn't risk them getting too far ahead.

He dialed Kane.

"Go ahead."

"They've been taken. My men are dead."

"Track them. And remember, they were dead already."

Leather's chest tightened. "Right now, I'd rather be one of them."

"Then there'd be no one left to save the others."

Hiroki and Koji hugged the ground as the gunfire raged just up the hill. Whoever was shooting at each other had an abundance of firepower and ammo, something they lacked.

They didn't dare intervene, or let themselves be spotted.

They wouldn't survive the night.

The gunfire fell silent, quickly replaced by shouting, then a few minutes later, footfalls in the forest, coming right toward them. Hiroki slithered back down the hill as best he could, Koji following as they tried to avoid being walked on top of.

But he didn't know where the gunmen were going. For all he knew, he could be retreating directly along their intended path.

It was pointless.

He grabbed Koji and halted his retreat, then pointed at a large tree to the left. They scrambled over to it and pressed against the thick trunk. He flipped his night-vision goggles back in place and peered out from around his cover.

And nearly fainted.

Not ten feet away were half a dozen armed men, leading five people, their hands bound behind them. He didn't recognize any of the hostages, but only one appeared Filipino, and three were Caucasian.

Why would they be here?

Then it occurred to him.

The gold.

His heart hammered as he realized the implications. There was no way these people would be here, at the exact location the map indicated, unless they too had the map. Could it be the Filipinos? They had the map as well, but if that were the case, why would there be Americans or Australians with them?

Regardless of why they were here, one thing was certain.

The terrorists who had just taken them hostage had no idea about the gold. If they did, they simply would have killed the hostages then stuck around to take the gold. The fact they had done neither suggested this was merely another sad case of foreigners taken hostage for ransom in the Philippines.

A twinge of pity made its presence felt.

Not enough to have him taking action.

His duty was clear.

He had to confirm the gold existed, and let Akira know.

Acton had managed to get his heart rate under control after he remembered his tactical breathing. He was as calm as could be expected, taking heart in the fact they were all still alive.

All except Leather's men.

He was devastated they were dead, of course, but he didn't know them. They weren't Leather's usual crew, men he had dealt with for years, men who weren't nameless, who had families and friends he had heard spoken of fondly.

The three unfortunate souls, lying dead up on the hill, were strangers to him, and it was horrible that he didn't feel as strongly about their loss as he should.

But it was human nature to mourn those close to you rather than strangers.

Yet they could have surrendered as well, but instead died defending people just as much strangers to them as they were to him. Did they have families? Loved ones who would miss them, would grieve for them properly?

He was certain they did.

And it made him feel all the more guilty.

He drew a long breath, calming his emotions that threatened to get the better of him as he struggled to remember the names of the fallen heroes he would never be able to thank.

When we get out of this, we'll make sure their families are taken care of.

It wasn't enough to assuage his guilt, yet it was the best he could do to honor their sacrifice.

He was the first into the old village, their vehicles still there. Laura was next followed by the whimpering pair of Tommy and Mai, with a muttering Bautista behind them. Two of the terrorists shot up the engines of all three vehicles, leaving his heart racing once again, Bautista's prayers at a fever pitch, and Mai openly sobbing with Tommy trying to console her, his own voice's trembling betraying his terror.

They never should have brought them.

Leather was right. It was too dangerous.

None of them should have come.

Yet they had just made the discovery of a lifetime.

Was it worth your life? The lives of those you love?

Obviously, no, though he couldn't let his actions be dictated by radical fundamentalists, and what they *might* do in the future. He had to live his life. They all did.

They were led through the trees to the road where two vehicles were parked. All five of them were squeezed into the back of the second vehicle, with Laura ending up in his lap, and Mai in Tommy's. Gags were unceremoniously tied around their mouths, adding to the misery of the cramped conditions.

And as they pulled away, he realized there would be no way for Leather to track them.

Their trucks had been rendered useless.

We're screwed.

As the gunfire faded behind him, their vehicles being disabled along with any hopes of pursuing them, Leather rushed toward the road. There had only been three vehicles in the old village—their vehicles. That meant the terrorists' transport had to be elsewhere, the likely location the road they had turned off of earlier in the day.

He reached the edge of the road and as expected, spotted two vehicles parked along the side. He scanned the area for hostiles, spotting none, and rushed toward the larger of the two, the one he suspected they'd put all the hostages in. Voices behind him had his pulse racing as he rolled under the vehicle and pulled out the satphone. He quickly dialed Kane, cursing at the single bar of battery power. He should have charged it earlier when he had the opportunity, yet he hadn't.

It was his fault.

And he just prayed it didn't cost the lives of those he was responsible for.

He pulled a zip tie from his utility belt, slipped it through the phone's belt clip then connected it to one of the tie rods of the vehicle.

Orders were snapped as the hostiles led his friends from the tree line and toward the waiting vehicles. He watched from underneath the truck, thankful it was at the rear, and watched the feet, his suspicions confirmed as the hostages were loaded into the back of the vehicle above him.

His eyes narrowed as he noticed something.

All of the terrorists were wearing matching boots.

What the hell?

The engine roared to life and pulled away a few moments later, leaving him exposed, though in the dark, with headlights blaring ahead, he decided staying frozen in place until they were out of sight was the best course of action. He rose and headed back to the village to see if he could salvage a vehicle.

For he might only have an hour left before the battery died on the phone.

The only hope he had of tracking them.

Philippine Army National Headquarters
Fort Bonifacio, Manila, The Philippines

"We have them."

Ocampo rose from his chair, a smile on his face as his cousin put down the phone. "Any difficulties?"

Cruz shook his head. "Two of our men were wounded, but they'll live."

"And the Americanos?"

"We eliminated the security team. The rest were unharmed."

Ocampo's smile spread. "And nobody knows about the gold?"

"Nothing was mentioned in the report, and they're heading into position now for the handoff. If they had seen anything, they'd have said something, or delayed their exit."

"But what if the hostages say something?"

"They've been gagged. They won't be able to say anything until after the handover."

"And then?"

"Then it will be too late. They'll all be dead."

Ocampo frowned. "Our friends aren't going to like that."

Park Hyatt Beijing

Beijing, China

Kane lay in bed, the surveillance camera overridden by a loop showing him sound asleep, the audio hearing a recording of his heavy breathing. Yet none of that was on his mind as he pressed his phone against his ear.

What the hell am I listening to?

He had heard loud bangs and scratching sounds, then shouts in a language he didn't recognize, then an engine and the creaking of what sounded like shocks on a car. The number that had called was Acton's satphone, but with no one responding on the other end, he had for a moment thought it might be a pocket-dial.

Yet the shouts ordering someone into a vehicle had quelled him of that notion.

And he smiled as he realized exactly what was going on.

Somebody had the phone with them, or had planted it in the vehicle.

They could track the phone.

He dialed into Langley with his laptop, fitting a headset into place. He gave his codename and password, and within less than a minute, was talking to his best friend and old high school buddy, Analyst Supervisor Chris Leroux.

"Hey buddy, did I interrupt anything tawdry?"

"I'm at work. You called me here. Remember?"

He grinned, always loving to tease his awkward friend. "The office wouldn't be the strangest place I've done inappropriate things. You should try it."

"Who says I haven't?"

His grin spread, his friend having met a great woman a couple of years ago who had dragged him from his shell.

Apparently even further than Kane had thought.

"You dawg! I want details. Better yet, I want pictures."

"Har-har. What's up?"

"Tap my cellphone. I'm connected with Professor Acton's satphone in the Philippines. They've been taken hostage, and I think they've activated their phone without the terrorists knowing."

"Just a sec."

He heard a keyboard furiously operated, then a grunt. "Mindanao. What are they? Stupid?"

"You don't want me to answer that. Are they moving?"

"Yeah, east, by the looks of it."

"Okay, track them as long as you can. See if you can get authorization for some eyes. I don't know how long the battery will last, and I'd hate to lose them."

"I'll see what I can do."

Maliit na Bahay, Mindanao, The Philippines

Hiroki waited for the sounds of the engines to fade in the distance before he dared relax. His heart was hammering, and he did feel bad for the people he had just watched get taken hostage. These were Islamic fundamentalists, who if they took a page from their ISIS brethren, would be raping the two women repeatedly before the night was through.

They should wipe them all from the face of the earth.

He wasn't a moral man. One didn't join the Yakuza if one was. Yet he did have a code of honor he lived by, and raping women wasn't a part of it, except in one way—he wouldn't hesitate to eviscerate a rapist.

They nuked us. Why aren't they nuking them?

The world had the vilest, most contemptible people in existence all concentrated in one area. Turn it all into glass, and solve a lot of the world's problems.

But the world's problems weren't his to solve. Not tonight. He turned to Koji. "Let's see if we can find that gold."

Koji grinned. "What are you going to do with your share?"

Hiroki eyed him as he climbed the hill. "Uhh, you actually think Akira's going to give us any?"

Koji shrugged. "If there's as much as they say up here, he'd never notice if a few gold bars went missing."

Hiroki paused, staring at his friend. "You better not let him hear you say things like that, or you'll lose more than a finger."

"I was just joking."

Hiroki resumed the climb. "Somehow I don't think so." He reached the top, his night-vision goggles revealing a rock-strewn landscape with some equipment near a large pile of stones.

He smiled at what appeared to be a hole in the side of the rockface, and what might lay on the other side. "I'd buy myself a one-way ticket to America, and lose myself in the streets of Los Angeles."

Koji punched him in the shoulder. "That's the spirit!"

Hiroki strode quickly to the hole, scanning in all directions with his goggles to make sure they were alone. He picked up a flashlight discarded near the entrance then flipped up his goggles before turning it on. "Here goes nothing." He climbed through the hole and shone his flashlight across the floor of the other side, his mouth filling with bile at the sight of so many dead.

Takashi's hiijiisan was a murdering bastard!

He had laid down some beatings in his career, but tonight was the first time he had actually killed anyone. It didn't bother him. He had seen dead bodies before, and those terrorists had been trying to kill him and his friends, succeeding twice. They deserved to die, and it didn't disturb him in the least.

But these bodies? These were innocent men, women, and children who were guilty of nothing but being born near a cave the Imperial Army needed.

No wonder they nuked us.

He finished his climb into the cave then spotted a large lamp to his right. He turned it on, flooding the area with light, the full extent of the horror revealed.

"Holy shit!" exclaimed Koji as he climbed through. "That kid's hiijiisan did this?"

"I guess so."

"I never would have thought someone in his family had the balls to do something like this."

Hiroki frowned. "Or was evil enough." He shook off the shivers, thoughts of what his own relations might have done in the war too disturbing to let take hold. "Let's go."

He led them deeper into the cave, and they didn't have to go far to find the treasure trove left untouched for over seventy years until today.

Yamashita's Gold.

His eyes bulged as he took in the sight of hundreds of crates, some opened revealing their precious contents.

"We're rich!" shouted Koji. "We're rich!"

Hiroki just stood, his mouth agape as he slowly absorbed their new reality. There was enough gold in here for every member of the Yakuza to never work again. Yet he knew Akira. He would never share it, though his stature would increase severalfold, and that would mean their lives would improve dramatically as they rode his coattails.

But they'd never really share in it.

Perhaps Koji is right.

He stepped over to one of the crates filled with gold bars, Koji's celebrations getting louder as he danced around the room. He picked up one of the bars, surprised at its heft.

Just one of these...

And a decision was made.

He grabbed Koji by the collar, ending his celebrations. "We need to call Akira and let him know."

"Of course! Can you imagine the women we're going to get? The cars? Life is going to be awesome!"

Hiroki stared at him. "Do you really want all that?"

"Of course!"

"And do you really think Akira is going to give it to you?"

Koji's joy slowly wiped away from his face. "Well, he'd give us something, wouldn't he?"

"Perhaps." Hiroki stared at the stacks of crates extending deeper into the cave, out of sight of his flashlight. "But I think you were right."

"What do you mean?"

Hiroki slapped a hand on the nearest crate of gold. "We each take a couple of these for ourselves."

Koji's eyes widened, fear on his face. "If he finds out, he'll kill us."

Hiroki grunted. "Then we'll have to make sure he never finds out. We take them tonight, hide them in the jungle, then come back for them. With this kind of money, they'll never find us."

A smile crept up the side of Koji's face as greed filled his eyes. "Why just two? Let's carry as much of this out of here as we can tonight. Nobody will ever know."

Hiroki's lust for wealth and power quickly overwhelmed any sense of fear at the risk they were about to take in betraying a Yakuza boss. With this kind of wealth, they could write their own ticket and live the lives they deserved. Akira was a fool, only in his position because of his father. *He* should be running the operation, not that arrogant idiot.

Yet he'd never get the chance.

And with this kind of money, he'd never *need* the chance.

"Are we agreed?"

Koji nodded vigorously. "Absolutely."

Excitement overcame Hiroki as he pulled out the satphone, and by the time he was crawling through the hole at the entrance so he could get a signal, he was as giddy as Koji.

You're rich!

He dialed Akira, his asshole of a boss answering immediately, the arrogant tone in his voice failing to curtail his happiness.

"Well, what the hell is going on there? We've been waiting!"

Hiroki gave the phone the finger, Koji slapping his hands over his mouth to keep from laughing. "We found it."

"You found it?" Akira's excitement was clear, and it had Hiroki grinning ear to ear once again.

"You have to see it, boss, it's unbelievable. The entire cave is filled with boxes of gold and jewels for as far as the eye can see."

He could hear Akira announce the news to the others in the room, cheers erupting. Akira finally quietened them down so he could talk. "What do you need to get it out of there?"

"Trucks and manpower. Lots of both. And weapons. Some people were here already. They were just taken hostage by terrorists. There's some equipment left here by them. We can use it to open up the entrance so we can move it out easier, but we're going to have to act fast. Those hostages could tell the terrorists about the gold to try and save their lives."

"Okay, get to work on that entrance. I'm going to make some calls and arrange trucks and men for tomorrow. Guard that gold with your lives, understood?"

"You got it, boss."

Akira ended the call and Hiroki shoved the phone in his pocket. He turned to Koji. "We might be getting visitors in the morning. Let's get as much of this out of here as we can."

Koji danced about some more then ripped his shirt off, spinning it over his head. "We're going to be rich, rich, rich!"

Hiroki smacked him on the back. "Only if you stop dancing and get to work!" He pointed at a pile of wood collected by the poor bastards taken away a short while ago. "Let's get a fire going. We'll need some light to work by if we're widening this hole."

"You got it!"

Koji went to work as Hiroki examined the jackhammer, never having handled one before.

Let's hope I don't gore myself the same day I became richer than the oyabun.

Leather cursed at the shot up engine, slamming the hood down. All three vehicles were totaled. He might get one working if he had the tools and the time, yet he had neither.

Laura and the others might be lost in less than an hour unless Kane could get his people to track them with a drone or satellite. A drone was unlikely. It would mean violating the airspace of an ally, and a satellite was also questionable. Retasking one was expensive. There would be coverage of the area as birds passed in their standard orbits, yet that might be intermittent.

Which meant it all might come down to him, and at the moment, either sprinting after them uselessly, or hoping he might hijack another passerby in the night, were his only two options.

Somebody shouted up the hill.

He drew his weapon and headed for cover, crouching behind a tree as he cocked an ear. There were two distinct voices, and they sounded happy. Celebratory.

Like they've just found billions in gold.

But who the hell was it? He had watched the entire group leave, including the right number of guns he had observed during the attack. It was possible there were others involved he hadn't seen, left behind to guard the cave, yet that didn't make sense either.

They would have to have known what was in the cave, and if they did, they wouldn't care about hostages. Why go to the trouble of getting ten or twenty million, when billions lay on the other side of a pile of rocks?

He made his way up the hill, and by the time he reached the top, the celebrating had settled down. The jackhammer fired up, eliminating any doubt as to why they were celebrating, and the glow of a fire flickered over the area. He crawled forward and spotted one working the rocks, and another stoking a large fire, the flame revealing full-body tattoos.

Yakuza! What the hell are they doing here?

Then a thought occurred to him.

And how did they get here?

A smile spread.

"I wish we had some booze."

Hiroki leaned on the jackhammer, exhausted. Manual labor had never been his thing, the most physical he ever got was beating a shop owner who didn't pay his protection money or repay a loan. And that usually only lasted a few minutes.

This?

This was insane.

He now had a new appreciation for just how tough a job construction was.

"I raided the minibar at the hotel. It's in my bag in the truck."

Koji grinned. "Shall we?"

Hiroki nodded. "One drink each. I don't want us so floor lickin' pissed that we don't get any gold out. And bring some water. This is going to be thirsty work."

"Got ya." Koji headed for their truck, parked on the road below, and was quickly lost in the darkness. Hiroki fired up the jackhammer again, wondering how long the propane-powered air compressor would last. He hoped long enough to widen the entrance so they could simply walk the crates out rather than push them through the small hole. It would be daylight before they knew it, and depending on how successful Akira was in arranging transport, they might have little time to move enough gold.

And that shit was heavy!

He frowned.

I wonder if the two of us can even carry a box of it.

He groaned at the thought. If they had to carry it in smaller batches, they might get very little in the end.

He cursed, pushing harder into the rock.

Then cursed again as he remembered the satphone needed charging. He turned off the jackhammer.

"Hey, Koji! Come back! I want you to plug in the phone!"

The rattle of the jackhammer provided Leather with all the cover he needed. He raced along the tree line, taking up a position to intercept the shirtless Yakuza heading out of the clearing. He might be going for a piss break, or he might be going for the vehicle they had to have arrived in.

A vehicle that the terrorists couldn't know about, otherwise he would have heard them shoot up its engine after the attack.

They wouldn't do it before, otherwise they would have ruined their ambush.

It might have been destroyed in that gunfire we heard earlier.

He suppressed a curse at the thought, and tossed his eyes upward, delivering a silent prayer for a change of fortune, for this day had gone horribly wrong in every way possible.

He positioned himself behind a tree, the Yakuza boldly striding past him, humming some happy bars, all his cares clearly gone, the only thing on his mind the gold his partner was working to ease access to.

Leather stepped forward, grabbing him from behind, placing him in a sleeper hold that had him uselessly struggling for less than a minute before passing out from lack of oxygen to the brain. Leather let him drop to the ground them flipped him over on his stomach. He zip-tied the man's hands and ankles, then shoved a handkerchief in his prisoner's mouth. He quickly searched the man's pockets, relieving him of a pistol and one spare mag, then a set of keys.

The jackhammer fell silent and there was a shout. He pulled his prisoner's unconscious form out of the direct line of sight of the clearing, then listened. Footfalls approached, the other man calling for someone named Koji.

Koji can't hear you.

Koji's partner strode confidently toward Leather's position, the possibility there was anyone else in the area clearly never occurring to the man. A foolish notion considering the din of the jackhammer and the air compressor, as well as the light from the roaring fire glowing in the night sky.

The man walked past his position and Leather stepped forward for a repeat of Koji's fate.

A twig snapped.

His opponent swung toward the sound, his arms rising into a fighting stance suggesting he might know what he was doing. Leather pressed forward, deflecting the man's arms with a sweep of his left, then took out his opponent's knee with a swift kick, a roar of agony erupting. Leather repositioned behind him, coiling his arm around the man's neck, and it was nap time within moments.

He bound his second prisoner then emptied his pockets, nearly shouting for joy at what he found.

A shiny new satphone.

The Lotus

Tokyo, Japan

Takashi had managed to sit up, the excitement in the room infectious, and the knowledge his hiijiisan had come through for him giving him hope his ordeal was finally over.

Akira dropped in the chair across from him, his smile wide. "So, your hiijiisan wasn't lying. Who knew?"

Takashi's chin sagged. "C-can I go now?"

Akira wagged a finger before picking up a shot of sake. "Not until we have the gold."

Takashi's heart sank and his eyes drooped closed. "But that wasn't the deal." His voice was barely a whisper.

"Your whining is killing my good mood. Somebody shut him up!"

His nurse strutted over and dropped into his lap, planting her lips on his, causing him to suck in a quick breath, infuriating his cracked ribs.

The pain was exquisite.

And ended his whining.

Maliit na Bahay, Mindanao, The Philippines

Leather double-checked his prisoners' bindings then activated the second man's iPhone. It was locked. He grabbed him by the hair and held his head back, putting the phone in front of his prisoner's face, the device unlocking a moment later. He swiped through the activated apps, spotting something unusual. He tapped, a map appearing with a red dot in the middle.

A tracker!

But who were they tracking? He zoomed out. In Japan.

He knelt down and smacked his latest acquisition. The man moaned and Leather removed the gag. He held up the phone. "What's this?"

The man blinked several times then stared at the phone. "Go to hell."

Leather jammed his thumb into a pressure point, a cry erupting. "I've got all day."

"Okay, okay! It's Takashi. We implanted him so he couldn't get away from us."

"Who's he?"

"He's the great-grandson of the man who did that." He jerked a chin up the hill.

"You mean the massacre?"

"Yes. He hid the treasure during the war."

"And what is Takashi to you?"

"He owes us money. If we don't get the gold, then he dies, and so does his great-grandfather." The man stared at him. "You better let us go or their blood is on your hands."

"Bollocks to that." He jammed the gag back in place then pulled up the settings used in the app and found the tracking frequency. He dialed Kane on his newly acquired satphone. The operator answered after two rings.

"It's Leather."

"I see you got another phone. Should I ask how?"

"Some Yakuza. I'll send you photos."

"Don't bother. I'm sending you Chris Leroux's number now. Do you know him?"

"I know of him." His phone vibrated and he checked the message, confirming it was from Kane and not some Yakuza scum. "Got it."

"Good. He's your handler on this. I'm about to go dark. Can you manage things?"

He could, if he had a destination. "I hope so."

"Good. These are my friends."

Leather tensed. "They're my friends too. I'll get them."

"I have no doubt."

Operations Center 2, CIA Headquarters

Langley, Virginia

CIA Analyst Supervisor Chris Leroux stood at the front of the operations center, the entire wall curving with dozens of displays, his team of experts manning their stations behind him as they processed the new intel just sent them by Cameron Leather, the head of security for a professor on his radar far too often.

Professor Laura Palmer.

And her impossibly unlucky husband, Professor James Acton.

He respected them both. Immensely, though didn't know them personally like Kane did. Kane was his best friend, one of his few friends. In fact, if it weren't for Kane, he would have no friends, and he'd certainly not be living with the amazing Sherrie White.

His circle was small, though larger than just a few years ago, when he was so isolated, his Facebook friends list was a sad collection of family members.

Yet now, his friends list was as equally pathetic as ever, as everyone he hung out with outside of work were CIA agents or foreign defectors, but his real-life friends might one day need a second hand to count.

Yet none of that bothered him now. Sherrie was the love of his life, Kane, his only friend in high school, was back in his life, and so was Kane's girlfriend, Lee Fang. He was still a nerd, but he now had the respect of his team, and his emergence from the cocoon of self-imposed exile was impressive.

And all of those in his life owed something to these two professors.

Which meant he would do whatever he could when asked.

Yet government assets were expensive, and these were civilians. Tapping data feeds that were already tapped was one thing, redeploying assets was something entirely different.

"These are the two I just incapacitated."

Leroux stared at the images Leather had just sent, eying the tattoos on display. "Yakuza?"

"That's my guess."

"Confirmed." Randy Child, his wunderkind computer expert, sent two Interpol files onto the display. "These guys look like they've lived lives their mothers would be proud of."

Leroux grunted. "Family reunions must be fun."

Sonya Tong, one of his senior analysts, stared at the images. "You know, I heard those tattoos actually cover *all* of their body."

Child's eyebrows shot up. "All?"

She nodded. "All."

"Huh. Does that mean they show each other their junk when comparing tattoos?"

Leather interrupted. "I'll ask them, if you want."

Child shrunk. "Sorry. Umm, you said you're in the Philippines. These two were flagged as possibly involved in an incident there yesterday, or I guess with the time difference, two days ago. I don't know. The day the professors arrived."

Leroux turned to him. "What kind of incident?"

"There was a shooting at the airport. One guard dead, another wounded. Witnesses say the shooter was Yakuza, but the Filipinos have said nothing, just that they're investigating. However, when they ran the check through Interpol, a known associates check was automatically performed by them, and they found your two guys traveled to Manila on the same day, along with two others."

Leroux frowned. "Did you just see the two, Colonel?"

"Yeah, but there was a firefight near here a while ago. They might have been taken out during that, or never left Manila."

"Well, watch your back. These guys look like they're bad news."

"So am I."

Leroux smiled. "I have no doubt."

"Listen, do you still have a lock on that phone?"

Leroux glanced at the display showing the tracked satphone planted on the kidnap vehicle. "Still going strong."

"Well, that won't last long. I'm going to see if I can find the vehicle that brought these guys here then pursue, but I won't be making good time. You need to get eyes on the HT's vehicle. That battery is going to die any minute."

"Copy that. You better find that vehicle, Colonel, just in case we can't come through for you."

"Roger that. Also, I found a tracking app on one of these guys. They say it's for some guy named Takashi. Apparently, he owes them money and his great-grandfather is the gentleman responsible for massacring the village when he hid the gold. I think he's in trouble. I'll send you the frequency. Maybe there's something you can do for him."

"I'll see what I can do."

"Copy that. Leather out."

The call ended and Leroux turned to Tong. "Any eyes yet?"

She shook her head. "Not for ten minutes."

Leroux cursed. "By then it might be too late." He chewed his cheek, staring at a map of the globe, the next satellite covering their op area highlighted. "Okay, the moment the bird is in range, I want everyone searching for the vehicle that took the professors. I'm going to talk to the Chief about retasking a bird."

Mindanao, The Philippines

Acton was wedged into the corner of the back seat. Laura was on his lap, repositioned so her back was against the door, her head resting on his shoulder. Tommy and Mai had managed the same on the opposite side, with Bautista wedged in the middle.

It was uncomfortable, yet he doubted anyone was focused on that fact.

The roads were horrible, the constant jolts from ruts and worse adding to the misery, each jarring shake irritating his wrists, though it was the gag that had become agonizing, his jaw stretched open, his mouth dry.

The only good thing that could be said was they weren't making good time.

Yet any time was better than Leather might manage. With their vehicles shot up, their head of security was left on foot, and no matter how good his conditioning, he couldn't keep up long enough for it to make a difference.

They were on their own.

Kane's plan had failed.

I just hope there's a Plan B.

He had little doubt Kane had reached out to his people at Langley, and if they were so inclined, they could track them. But only if they could find them. It was dark, they were in a thick jungle, and it had been almost an hour since they were taken.

The search radius was impossibly large.

And even if they managed to find them, then what?

They could send in a team to rescue them, or notify the Filipinos to do the same, but how long would that take? And by then, they might be shuffled somewhere else.

Or worse.

He kissed the top of Laura's head, his chest tight at the thought of what might happen to her and Mai when they arrived at their ultimate destination. There were terrorist groups here that had aligned themselves with ISIS. That fact made death his second-worst fear.

Infidel women were fair game according to the interpretation of the Koran that these monsters followed.

If they were rescued, then all would be well, though he couldn't count on that. Escape was unlikely, and risky. Kane was right in that regard. They had let themselves be captured, now they had to make sure these people thought the ransom was going to be paid.

And only if they all remained untouched.

They had the money to pay the ransom. That wasn't an issue, though it could take time, and he hated the idea of financing these monsters. Yesterday he might have even criticized the idea, though now that he had a different perspective, where the people he loved the most were the faceless hostages, his attitude had dramatically changed, the hypocrisy not lost on him.

What about the gold?

That might speed up things, though perhaps for the worse. If they had the gold, then they wouldn't need the ransom.

Which means they wouldn't need us.

They'd be dead the moment the gold was confirmed.

He glanced at the others, wondering how he might warn them to keep their mouths shut.

It just might mean their lives.

Director Morrison's Office, CIA Headquarters

Langley, Virginia

"What's on your mind, Chris?"

Chris Leroux closed the door to Leif Morrison's office, the National Clandestine Service Chief for the CIA. Morrison indicated for him to sit, and Leroux dropped into the chair. "I need to retask a bird."

Morrison's eyebrows rose slightly and he leaned back in his chair, steepling his fingers in front of him. "What for?"

"It looks like Islamic terrorists have kidnapped Professors Acton and Palmer, along with two other subjects we're familiar with, one Thomas Granger and one Mai Trinh, along with a local Filipino professor."

Morrison sighed, shaking his head. "They should make a TV series out of those two."

"Who would star as you?"

"Kevin Costner. I think he could pull off my rugged good looks."

Leroux chuckled. "I'm sure he'd give it a hell of a try."

"Any ransom demands yet?"

Leroux shook his head. "No. The fact they were taken rather than killed suggests that's their intent. My guess is they're going to move them around so we'll have a harder time finding them. That's why we need to enhance our coverage of the area before that happens."

"Go ahead and do it." Morrison leaned forward. "How'd you find out? I just got off the phone with the Pentagon about this." His eyes narrowed. "And they didn't know who was kidnapped."

Leroux stared at him. "Sorry, what?"

"The Pentagon just called. We've been asked to help in a matter in the Philippines. I assume it's the same thing. Did they contact you?"

Leroux shook his head. "No. Kane put us onto it. Colonel Cameron Leather is on the scene. He contacted us via satphone immediately after the kidnapping."

"Interesting. When did this happen?"

"Less than an hour ago."

Morrison's eyebrows shot up. "Very interesting. The Vice Commander of the Philippine Army contacted the Pentagon through channels, requesting US assistance in rescuing a group of hostages taken less than an hour ago. He claims they were taken by the Moro Islamic Liberation Front on Mindanao."

"I think we can safely say we're talking about the same incident."

"I think so."

Leroux chewed his cheek for a moment, processing this new information. "It's remarkably quick notice, isn't it? I mean, how do they already know? We had someone at the scene and we just found out. And if they started making phone calls, that takes time."

"We have hotlines with them, but it still smells fishy to me."

"What are we—I mean collectively—going to do?"

"We already have presidential approval to go in and rescue the hostages. It'll be a joint operation between US and Filipino forces. The President doesn't want to risk losing them in the jungle. The intel is so fresh, we might be able to get them out this time before they get a chance to squirrel them away."

"Well, Leather planted a satphone on one of the hostiles' vehicles, but the battery is going to run out at any minute. If we can't locate them in time via satellite, we may still lose them."

"My briefing indicates the Filipinos have people embedded in some of the cells there. They're confident they'll be able to find out where they are before our Spec Ops team is in position."

Leroux shifted in his chair. "Anyone we know?"

"Some of Bravo Team are in Taiwan right now. They just finished up an op and are heading back here in a couple of hours. They're being notified now."

"That's good. They know the professors, so won't stop at anything to protect them. I'm a little concerned that if this isn't handled properly, the terrorists could eliminate the hostages before they can be rescued."

"That's why this is being taken seriously. The USS Ronald Reagan is in the South China Sea right now. They'll be providing support. And the President has insisted that we have the lead."

"And the Filipinos agreed to this?"

"They weren't happy, but yes."

Leroux shook his head. "Why does my gut tell me something is wrong here?"

Morrison frowned. "When your gut gets nervous, things tend to go to shit in a hurry."

Ching Chuan Kang Air Base
Taichung, Taiwan

"I call bullshit on that."

Sergeant Carl "Niner" Sung rolled his head to the side, giving the massive Sergeant Leon "Atlas" James the stink-eye. "Oh really? And you're an expert in plasma physics?"

Atlas' impossibly deep voice rumbled in response. "Just as much an expert as you are, little man."

"So what you're saying is that YouTube is lying to me? To the world?"

Atlas' head tipped forward, his eyes looking up at Niner. "You got this moronic idea from YouTube?"

"Yes." Niner folded his arms. "You can learn a lot from YouTube."

"I'm sure you can. Perhaps you should look up some videos on why you can't trust everything you see on the Internet."

Command Sergeant Major Burt "Big Dog" Dawson popped a grape in his mouth, the subject fruit the trigger for the current conversation.

He was the senior NCO of the group, all elite Special Forces, members of 1st Special Forces Operational Detachment–Delta, or Delta Force to the civvies out there. They had just finished up an op, the location of which perhaps a dozen people on the face of the planet knew, and were heading back home. He was eager to see his fiancée, Maggie. It had been too long. Two weeks pre-positioned near the target area, waiting for word that their subject had arrived, then a rapid insertion to capture him then exfiltrate.

It had been a success, though two weeks of absolute and complete boredom had been tough, especially since they weren't allowed to communicate with their loved ones.

It was simply too important to capture this particular target.

He held up a grape. "You're telling me, that if I put this grape in that microwave over there"—he pointed the orb toward a microwave that would look in place on Stranger Things—"that it will start to arc, and that those beams of light shooting out of it are actually plasma, like in the sun."

"Exactly."

Sergeant Will "Spock" Lightman threw up an eyebrow. "I'm with Atlas. I call bullshit on that."

"Oh, yee of little faith." Niner held out a hand. "Toss me one of those."

Sergeant Eugene "Jagger" Thomas reached out and yanked the bowl with the grapes away from Niner. "But these are tasty. I don't want any going to waste."

Niner gave him a look as Jagger downed several. "Check those monster lips of yours, I think you lost one in them before they reached your mouth."

Jagger blew him a kiss.

Atlas reached over and yanked a grape off the stem then rolled it across the table toward Niner. "Okay, hotshot, let's see this. A Benjamin says nothing happens but the wasting of a perfectly good grape."

"Deal." Niner grabbed the grape and drew his knife. He sliced the tip off one end, then cut it almost all the way through. He grabbed his glass of water and walked over to the sink, dumping its contents before opening the microwave. He put a plate inside, then the grape splayed open on top of it, then flipped over the glass and covered the grape. "Ready?"

Everyone gathered around and he cranked the ancient dial, selecting three minutes, then hit the button to turn on the outdated appliance.

And nothing happened.

"Told you," rumbled Atlas.

"Patience, muscle boy."

Suddenly, flashes of light and what appeared to be lightning bolts sprung from the grape, dancing along the sides of the glass, the display unbelievably cool.

"Holy shit!" exclaimed Jagger. "He was right!"

"I don't understand why you guys always doubt me."

Atlas gave him a quick glance before returning his attention to the microwave's special effects show. "Because you're almost always full of shit."

A loud bang had everyone jumping back, the glass on the front of the microwave cracking as Niner leaped forward to turn it off.

"What the hell was that?" asked Jagger as Niner opened the door, revealing a shattered water glass and a smoking grape. "Are you trying to kill us?"

Niner shrugged. "I guess I left it in too long."

"Ya think?"

"Hey, it's not like the grape came with a manual or anything."

Dawson sat back down, jabbing a finger at the microwave. "You're paying for that. Our Taiwanese hosts aren't going to be too pleased."

Niner touched the grape, quickly recoiling. "Hot!"

Atlas rolled his eyes. "You need to see a head doctor."

"Been there, done that. He committed himself after talking to me."

The door opened and the Taiwanese sergeant assigned as their liaison entered. "There were reports of an, umm, explosion? Is everything all right?"

Niner patted the top of the microwave. "I think the Chinese just tried to kill us." He pulled it out from the counter and looked at the back. "Yup. Made in China."

The sergeant's eyebrows shot up. "I must report this!"

Dawson prevented an international incident and a mountain of paperwork. "No, he's just joking. The idiot put something in the microwave he shouldn't. Send us the bill and I'll make sure he pays it."

The sergeant bowed. "No problem." His eyes narrowed. "Don't they tell you not to put metal in the microwave in America?"

Atlas grunted. "It was a grape."

The sergeant's eyes shot wide. "Even stupider!"

Laughter erupted as the sergeant grinned then left, closing the door behind him. Dawson's phone vibrated and he held up a finger, silencing the room.

"Hello?"

"Zero-One, Control Actual. I've got new orders for you."

Operations Center 2, CIA Headquarters

Langley, Virginia

"Leather is on the move."

The secure door closed behind Leroux with a hiss as he rejoined his team in the impressive operations center. "So, I guess he found the Yakuza's vehicle."

Child nodded. "Yup. And evidently the terrorists didn't."

"And that guy he said the Yakuza were tracking? Anything on that?"

Child pointed at the screen. "He's in Tokyo. Looks like some nightclub called The Lotus. I ran a check on it and it's Yakuza owned."

Tong clasped her hands behind her neck. "I don't think he's there for a night out on the town."

Leroux agreed. "He's probably their guest until the gold is delivered. With that no longer happening, they'll probably kill him." He frowned, dropping into his chair. "But he's not our concern."

Tong's eyes shot wide. "You're not suggesting we just let them kill him."

Leroux rolled his head to the side, giving her a look. "Have you ever known me to just let some innocent die?"

Tong flushed, her inappropriate crush on him still in bloom. "Umm, no."

"Right. We need to pass this on to the police. Interpol."

Child spun in his chair, staring up at the ceiling. "Agent Reading?"

Leroux nodded. "Get him for me."

Reading Residence

Whitehall, London, England

"You know, I don't think there's anything better than a good moo shu."

Interpol Agent Hugh Reading's son, Spencer, shook his head. "Give me a good curry any day." He jabbed a fork toward his father's dish. "Too many vegetables. You'll be hungry in an hour."

"Bollocks. The key is to ask for extra pork and pancakes."

"You'll get fat."

Reading patted his stomach, a few pounds added over the years, but nothing he was embarrassed about. "I'm getting old. I'm allowed."

His son shrugged. "Hey, I'm just saying, one day you're a gladiator, the next day you're Russell Dough."

Reading snorted. "That's mean."

"I know. And that's the world we live in." Spencer pushed his plate away, leaning back in his chair and patting his perfectly flat stomach.

"That's enough for me. I've got physical training in the morning, and I don't want to be hurling."

Reading rose. "I'll put the remainder in a container for you."

Spencer waved him off. "Sit, finish your food. I'll take care of it."

Reading sat, giving his son the eye. "I thought I wasn't supposed to finish?"

His son laughed. "Bugger off! You're not fat."

Reading's phone vibrated on the table beside him and he checked the call display, his eyes narrowing at the unknown number. He put down his fork and swiped his thumb. "Hello?"

"Hello, Agent Reading, this is Chris Leroux."

Reading tensed as he recognized who was on the other end of the line, the fact the CIA was calling him never a good sign. "What have they done now?"

Acton and Laura were his two best friends in the world, and they were always getting into trouble, too often dragging him along with them. If the CIA was on the line, they were likely neck-deep in something they shouldn't be.

"They're in a situation that I can't talk about, however, rest assured, we're taking action. The reason I'm calling you is actually official business. I have a piece of intel I want to hand over responsibility for, without it coming back to us."

"And you thought of me. I'm touched."

Leroux chuckled. "You have proven trustworthy in the past."

"No problem. What is it you need me to take care of?"

"We came across a tracker. Apparently, a young man named Takashi is being held by the Yakuza in Tokyo. He has a subdermal tracker implanted. I'm sending you the details now. It might be nice if someone in law enforcement saved his life. He'll probably be dead by morning."

Reading's phone vibrated with Leroux's message as he frowned. "You're sure of this?"

"As sure as I can be without getting involved. I recommend you use your contacts within Interpol to get the Tokyo police to rescue him in the next few hours, otherwise it will be too late."

"Very well. Should I call you back to let you know what happens?"

"I'll probably know before you."

Reading laughed. "I find that notion terrifying." He became serious. "And Jim and Laura? Will they be okay?"

"All I can promise is we'll do our best."

Mindanao, The Philippines

Acton jerked forward then back as their vehicle came to an abrupt halt. The soldiers climbed out and cigarettes were lit and leaks taken. Conversations were had, none of which he understood, and if they were of any importance, the gagged Bautista couldn't warn them regardless.

He stared up at the night sky, barely visible through the trees, and wondered if Kane's people were watching, a rescue already underway.

He doubted it.

At least the latter part. They might very well be watching, but any rescue attempt was likely days away. It took time to cut through red tape, to organize things, to mount an operation. And if demands were made, people at the other end would weigh their options.

Who would decide if the ransom was paid?

He had already decided it had to be. Precedent be damned. It had already been set, and he had too many lives that were important to him to protect. Yet it wasn't his decision alone. It was Laura's money, no matter how much she said it was both of theirs, but even if it wasn't, she had a say too.

Though he knew what she would say, merely for the fact Tommy and Mai were with them.

She'd say to pay it.

And it would be, eventually, as long as nothing went wrong.

But things always went wrong, and his greatest fear was that something would happen to the women in the meantime, or that one of them would be made an example of to encourage payment, to show they were serious.

Someone shouted, pointing under their car. One of their captors rushed forward then dropped to the ground, climbing under the vehicle. He shouted, then reemerged, holding up a satphone, the glow indicating it was connected to a call.

Leather!

He must have attached it to the undercarriage somehow. Renewed hope surged through him as there was only one reason to do such a thing.

So it could be tracked.

That meant the CIA knew exactly where they were.

One of the men stepped forward, yanking their door open then the gag out of Acton's mouth. "Explain this!"

"Explain what? You've had us tied up the entire time. You know we couldn't do it."

"If you didn't do it, someone else did! Who else was with you?"

"Nobody!"

The man drew his pistol and pressed it against Mai's head. She cried out, cringing into the corner as Tommy roared at him, pushing his head in the way to try and block any shot. He was pistol-whipped for his efforts, blood trickling from the resulting wound.

"Listen, I swear, I don't know how that got there." He tested his luck. "Whoever did it obviously knows where we are. Why don't you just let us go? We don't know who you are. We've never seen your faces. Just leave us here and go. No one gets hurt."

A smack with the back of the man's hand was the response. "Enough!" He tossed the phone on the ground and stomped the heel of his leather boot onto it, crushing the device. The door slammed shut and the terrorists returned to the vehicles. Within minutes, they were far from the phone.

And any ability to track them.

Now we're really screwed.

USS Ronald Reagan
South China Sea

Command Sergeant Major Dawson stared at the screen at the front of the briefing room, his team sitting around the table while they were brought up to date by Leroux remotely.

"This is their last known location before the phone went dead. We were expecting the battery to die, though audio suggests the phone was actually discovered. We were able to hear Professor Acton's voice, so we know at least he's alive. We also heard a woman crying, though we don't know if that was Professor Palmer or Miss Trinh. We believe it was Miss Trinh."

"Any eyes on the area?" asked Niner.

"We didn't have a visual until after the phone was discovered. We're searching now. With it being the middle of the night, we're hoping to get lucky as traffic should be at a minimum. But there's a problem."

Dawson rolled his eyes. "There always is. What is it this time?"

"The Filipinos are already mobilizing. They've sent several hundred men into the area."

Atlas growled. "Why the hell did they go and do that?"

"They claim they're searching for the hostages, but as far as we're concerned, all they're doing is letting everyone know they're coming. Radio chatter is way up, and MILF seems to be repositioning to repel them."

Dawson shook his head in disbelief. "This makes no sense. Didn't our advisors tell them this was an idiotic move?"

"They did, but apparently the orders came from the Vice Commander of their army himself. The Pentagon thinks he must have some connection to one of the hostages."

Jagger pursed his lips. "Does he know the professors?"

"Intel says they've never crossed paths, and in fact, we have no evidence to suggest the Filipinos have any idea who the hostages are."

Looks were exchanged around the table. Dawson leaned forward. "We haven't told them?"

"No. We've said we're trying to ID them from travel records."

"So, they have no idea about the phone we've been tracking."

"No."

Dawson leaned back in his chair and folded his arms. "Something's going on here. I don't like to go into an op not trusting my supposed allies. And I've worked with the Filipinos before. They're way smarter than this."

Niner agreed. "It looks like a come and get me op."

"What do you mean?" asked Leroux.

"Make a bunch of noise, attract the attention of your targets, then invite them to a party. Go in with heavy firepower and wipe them out. Hostages be damned." Niner shrugged. "If they don't care about them, that is."

It sounded far-fetched to Dawson, though the evidence in front of them would suggest otherwise. "Could this be a rogue op?"

Leroux responded. "How? He's the Vice Commander. That's only two steps down from the President."

Atlas glanced at Dawson. "Maybe we should call the President?"

Leroux disagreed. "Not with relations the way they are. He's liable to scrap the joint operation and we'll never see our people again. No, we have to assume this is legit, and try to get our people before the mess they're creating gets too thick."

Dawson stared at the map, noting the location of the kidnapping. "The initial report from Leather indicated they had found some sort of Japanese treasure?"

"Yamashita's Gold."

"Do we know who knows?"

"The hostages and apparently the Yakuza. Other than that, no."

Dawson chewed his cheek for a moment. "What if the Filipinos know?"

"Wouldn't they just go in and secure the area?" asked Niner.

"That's what you'd think they'd do. But what if they found some American and British scientists sitting on their gold?"

Atlas shrugged. "Kick them out. It's their territory."

"Is it? Isn't this part of some autonomous region?"

Leroux clarified. "Yes, but they still come under Filipino jurisdiction ultimately. And either way, your professors don't belong there."

Dawson regarded the others who knew them so well. "No, they don't, but our professors are noisy people when they want to be. Most Westerners are if they don't get their way."

"What are you suggesting?"

"I'm suggesting that someone knows exactly what's there, and the fact the professors were there, even if they don't know who they are specifically."

"Someone? Don't you mean the Filipino government?"

Dawson shook his head. "No. I think the government has no clue what's there. I think some*one* knows, likely the Vice Commander, and this is all a ruse to clear the area."

There was a pause before Leroux replied. "You mean they kidnapped our people?"

Dawson shrugged. "Leather said they appeared to be MILF or equivalent, but he reported a drone earlier in the day that appeared military. I think it's a distinct possibility that this is rogue, they kidnapped our people to get us involved to legitimize their operation, and are using it to send a contingent into the area to take whatever is in that cave, while creating a distraction that will have every MILF regular charging toward wherever it is they're leading us."

"If that's the case, Sergeant Major, then perhaps we should withdraw."

Niner slammed his fist on the table. "Bullshit!"

"Exactly!" rumbled Atlas, the others agreeing vigorously.

As did Dawson. "To hell with that. Someone has our friends, and we intend to extract them."

Mindanao, The Philippines

Their vehicle skidded to a halt and their captors climbed out then opened the rear doors. Laura was grabbed by the arm and hauled out, then Acton was beckoned to follow. He complied, his entire body cramping as he struggled to exit with his hands bound. He finally succeeded and was shoved out of the way as Bautista was pulled out. Acton checked to see Tommy and Mai standing on the other side of the vehicle.

One of the men pointed into the jungle. "Walk that way," he said, his voice low.

Acton, still free of his gag, stared warily into the dark. "Why?"

A rifle butt slammed into his gut, doubling him over.

"No questions. Walk, or die. Your choice."

"How far?" The rifle was raised again and Acton spun away. "Okay! Okay! No questions!"

"Just walk to the village. It's not far."

He stepped from the road and into the trees, the rest following, and as they picked their way in the darkness, he heard the vehicles leave, back in the direction they had come from.

They were alone.

He stopped and turned to face Laura. He leaned forward and grabbed her gag with his teeth and pulled it loose. He did the same with Tommy then Bautista, Tommy taking care of Mai. As they stood for a moment, gaining their breaths, he gave them the warning he had been dying to give.

"Whatever you do, don't mention the gold. The moment they find out, we're dead."

"Why?" asked Tommy.

"Because then ransom means nothing to them. We have to be united on this, no matter how scared any of us get. The moment they know about the gold, we're dead. We have to make sure they know we'll pay the ransom, but only if none of us are hurt. Everybody agreed?"

A round of nods.

"Good."

Tommy stared about wide-eyed. "Now what do we do?"

Acton wasn't certain about anything. "We could go back to the road and try to hike it out. We'll have to get these bindings off first, but it might be the safest thing."

"But won't they be expecting us?" asked Laura.

He paused. She was right. This was a handoff. One group delivering them into the hands of another, probably the first of many exchanges. Why it wasn't done in person, he wasn't certain. Perhaps it was a security measure. If they didn't see one another, they could never betray one another. And if this was an exchange, and they didn't show up at this village in the next few minutes, a search party would be sent for them, leading to one or more of them punished or worse.

He sighed.

"I think you're right. We have to follow their orders."

"Are you insane!" hissed Bautista. "They're Islamic terrorists! You would voluntarily hand yourself over to them? Your wife? This young girl?"

Acton bristled. "There's nothing voluntary about this, Buwan. They're expecting us. If we don't show up, they're sending guns after us. We can't outrun them. They know this area, they have vehicles. We wouldn't stand a chance."

Bautista's shoulders slumped, resignation on his face, though he remained silent.

Acton turned to the others. "Are we all agreed?"

Laura nodded firmly, supporting him as always, though the others were more reluctant.

"Good. And remember, no mention of the gold, not even among ourselves." He drew a deep breath then exhaled heavily. "Once more unto the breach."

He headed deeper into the jungle, away from the road and its slim chance of freedom, and toward the glimmers of life ahead. The sounds of domesticated animals reached his ears along with a few whispered voices.

They were nearly at the village.

He stepped through the final stand of trees and emerged into a large cleared area, several dozen huts visible, lit by small untended fires leftover from earlier in the evening. The village appeared asleep.

He stopped.

Shouldn't they be awake? Shouldn't they be expecting them?

A horrible thought occurred to him, and he turned to urge them back into the jungle.

We're not expected at all!

Someone shouted behind him and he froze. Another shout, then another, and what was a moment ago a slumbering village was no more as he turned to face the reality that might not have been.

Yet why? Why would they hand them off without informing the other group?

None of it made sense, and none of it mattered now as they were quickly surrounded by armed men, leaving little doubt this wasn't some innocent village of farmers, but a village of farming terrorists.

"They want to know why we're here."

Bautista's English translation had one of them rushing forward, jamming his AK-47 in Acton's face. "American?"

Acton nodded. "Yes."

The man eyed Acton's bound hands. "Why you here?"

"We were told to walk here. By your people."

The man leaned over to look behind them. "What people?"

"Back at the road. They kidnapped us and brought us here. They told us to walk through the trees until we reached you."

A local dialect was exchanged rapidly between the men, then they were all grabbed and forced to the center of the village where they were shoved to their knees near one of the fires.

"What's going on?" asked Laura in a whisper, her head down, trying not to draw any undue attention to herself.

Acton kept his own head down, taking in as much as he could from his peripheral vision. "I don't know, but I don't think these people had any idea we were coming."

"Don't they have radios?"

"I would think so, but I guess whoever kidnapped us didn't tell these guys."

And as he watched, he noticed something that brought back a memory he had forgotten.

All these men were in shabby footwear, or none at all.

And not a one of them had leather boots like their kidnappers.

Like those who might have operated the drone from earlier in the day.

The drone Leather had been convinced was military.

"I've got a bad feeling about this."

Philippine Army National Headquarters
Fort Bonifacio, Manila, The Philippines

"What's happening?"

Ocampo's voice was low, his presence in the command center already raising eyebrows among the few staff brought in to run the operation. Even the Americans had been kept out, security reasons cited. His cousin had said they weren't happy about it, but had agreed when they were told they could have control of the mission and the command center would merely be observing.

Cruz glanced over at him. "They've just been handed off. Comm traffic from the area just went up. I guess they're trying to figure out who delivered them into their hands."

Ocampo chuckled. "It must have been a shock."

"Our contacts tell us they think they're being set up, and our operatives are fueling those rumors. The force we sent in earlier is making their presence known. MILF is gearing up for a fight and starting to reposition their forces."

"What did the Americans say when they found out about the troops you sent in?"

"They weren't pleased. They feel we've tipped them off."

"Fools."

Cruz grunted. "Don't underestimate them."

"But they've bought it, haven't they? I mean, you said they're sending in a Special Ops team."

"They have. They're already in the air. They'll be rendezvousing with our choppers for insertion."

Ocampo folded his arms. "Good. With all this going on, we should be able to secure the…site…and begin removal, assuming it's there."

Cruz regarded him for a moment. "It better be, or it's your head."

One of his men approached with a folder. "General, we've identified some of the hostages." He handed over the folder. "We crosschecked their passports with immigration. Two Americans, a Brit, and a Vietnamese national. The other is a local professor."

Cruz's eyebrows rose. "An odd combination." He dismissed the soldier then sat at his laptop, typing for a moment. He leaned back. "Professor James Acton. He's an archaeologist, well respected. Looks like he's been busy." He typed some more. "And Professor Palmer. She's an archaeology professor as well." He folded his arms and scratched his chin. "These two are high profile. The other two are just kids in their twenties." He handed the file to Ocampo who quickly scanned it then paused, his eyes narrowing.

"They arrived at Terminal Four."

"So?"

"So, that means they probably arrived on a private charter. It says here they came direct from the US. That means private jet. They're either rich or well-funded." He stared at his cousin. "This could be a problem."

Operations Center 2, CIA Headquarters

Langley, Virginia

"The satellite is in position."

Leroux pointed at the display without looking at Tong. "Bring it up." The display flickered and the image was replaced with footage of the area, their assets already inbound displayed with associated metadata. "Show me their last known location."

Tong tapped at the keyboard, a section of the jungle highlighted then zoomed in on. "This is where we lost the satphone signal."

"Okay, let's try some filters."

"What do you want?"

"Well, if I'm driving in the jungle at night, I want headlights. Let's see what we find."

Tong went to work and moments later the display updated with a disheartening sight.

Dozens of vehicle headlights were visible, most headed east.

Child cursed. "We're never going to find them like this."

Leroux agreed. "As soon as the Filipinos sent those forces in, every cell in the area activated."

Child popped something up on the display. "Check this out. It looks like there's a heavy engagement in the northeast."

Leroux's eyes narrowed as he stepped closer to the display. "How far is that from our last known position?"

"Almost a hundred miles. There's no way they got them there by car."

"Chopper?" suggested Tong.

"Possible, but I highly doubt MILF has any at their disposal." Leroux scratched his neck. "Why the hell would they engage them there?"

"Distraction? They're hoping to attract fighters to the decoy so it makes it easier for us to rescue the hostages at the real target?"

Leroux nodded. "Could be. Risky, and it could just panic our hostage-takers." He sighed. "They should have just stayed at their base and let Delta do its job."

Child spun in his chair. "It would have been nice and clean."

Leroux turned to face his team, jerking his thumb over his shoulder at the displays. "Well, with this Charlie-Foxtrot happening, it's going to be anything but."

Tong raised a finger, drawing his attention. "Sir, the Pentagon just relayed a message from the Philippines. They've located our people."

Leroux's eyes narrowed. "Already?" He joined her and read the message. "Get me Bravo One."

Over Mindanao, The Philippines

Dawson checked his gear for the umpteenth time as the Sikorsky SH-60 Sea Hawk ferried his team from the USS Ronald Reagan into the field of battle. For he feared it would be that. This was no longer a simple extraction. His last update from the Pentagon was that the Filipinos had sent in a large contingent and engaged a known MILF encampment. Now the entire island was going apeshit.

His words, not theirs.

"Bravo Zero-One, this is Control Actual."

Command of the mission had been ceded to the CIA, as they were familiar with all the parties involved, and how they were likely to react. The last thing they needed was brass in DC thinking these were your typical scared civilians just waiting to be rescued. If he knew the professors—and he did—they'd be plotting their escape, and the moment the shit hit the fan, they'd be taking action.

It meant civilians on the battlefield, possibly engaging the enemy, and possibly in the line of fire.

It had to be accounted for, and his team and Leroux's had worked together on numerous occasions, too many of those dealing with the professors.

Dawson activated his comm. "Go ahead, Control."

"We have an exact location for your targets. Coordinates are being transmitted now."

"Copy that." He switched channels so he could talk to their pilot, Sergeant Zach "Wings" Hauser. "One-Two, confirm receipt of new coordinates for drop, over."

"Got them, BD. Adjusting course."

Dawson switched back to Leroux. "Did you say exact? I was expecting a little hunting."

"So were we. Our hosts have operatives embedded within some of the cells. I guess we got lucky."

Dawson grunted. "Well, I have a theory about that."

"Does it involve who you can trust?"

"It would appear we think alike."

"Just watch your back, Zero-One."

"I always do. Zero-One, out." Dawson rose and headed for the cockpit, smacking Wings on the shoulder. "Can this heap go any faster?"

Wings glanced at him. "Yeah, but our allies' crates can't."

"Good. Punch it, Chewie."

Philippine Army National Headquarters
Fort Bonifacio, Manila, The Philippines

"Sir, our pilots have just reported that the Americans have broken formation. They've increased speed."

General Cruz cursed as he slammed his fist on the desk. "Increase speed to match!"

The lieutenant providing the update appeared terrified with the response he was forced to provide. "I'm sorry, sir, they can't. They're already at their maximum speed."

"Do the Americans have an explanation?"

"They've told us to stand by."

"How much ahead of us will they be?"

"They'll reach the target location ten minutes ahead."

Cruz cursed again, dismissing the lieutenant with the flick of his wrist. Ocampo rose from his chair and leaned over his cousin's desk, his voice low. "Why would they do that? Do you think they know?"

Cruz eyeballed him. "How the hell could they? We're the only two who know what's going on."

"Our men that took them know."

"What do they really know? They don't know about the gold, and they don't know about the ultimate plan. Their mission is over. Hell, our team that's inbound doesn't even know about the hostages! They think they're raiding a camp. We have total containment on this."

"What if one of the hostages talked? If they told our team about the gold, then can we really trust them?"

Cruz paused, staring at him for a moment. "I never thought of that." He slammed his fist on his desk again. "We've been betrayed!"

Reading Residence

Whitehall, London, England

"We've located the signal. It's a nightclub called the Lotus. It's a Yakuza operation like you suspected."

Hugh Reading frowned, tapping his pencil against his notepad. "When are you going in?"

"We're trying to get a warrant now. It's delicate. They have ears everywhere. If they find out we're coming, they'll remove the tracker and either move the target, or kill him."

Reading leaned back in his chair, clasping his free hand behind his neck. "I understand. Keep me posted."

"Will do."

Reading ended the call, tossing his phone on the table.

Spencer folded his arms. "Sometimes I wonder why we need warrants."

"You're a copper. You know why. It prevents abuse of power."

"Yeah, but when someone's life is in danger—"

"Then you go in. That's allowed. The problem here is that the information we have is too thin to go in without a warrant. There's no real evidence that this is real. For all we know, it could be tracking someone's set of keys."

"You know, there's an app for that."

"Of course there is. The next thing you know, there'll be one to track my bollocks."

"Actually…"

Reading rolled his eyes.

"Why are you dealing with the Japanese police? Doesn't Interpol have people there that can handle this?"

"We have people, but Interpol isn't like in the movies. We don't have armed agents running around the world. We're just an administrative branch that has members of various police forces working for it. We're a fancy liaison office for the most part. We do investigations, but the real arrests are all local."

"Sounds boring."

Reading sighed. "You have no idea."

His son regarded him. "Do you ever regret leaving Scotland Yard?"

"Every bloody day."

Mindanao, The Philippines

Leather's foot eased off the gas as he heard something overhead. His eyes widened and he jammed on the brakes then cut the engine. The rotors of a helicopter beating the air above were unmistakable.

And close.

The aircraft raced past his position, barely above the treetops, though out of sight, the canopy of trees overhead blocking it from view.

Yet he knew his airframes well enough to know it was a Black Hawk-class helicopter.

Definitely not Filipino. Not yet.

A purchase was underway for Polish-built Black Hawks, but they hadn't been delivered yet. This had to be the Americans, which meant Kane's people had come through.

And the fact they had just overflown his position could only mean one thing.

I'm on the right track.

He fired up the engine and hammered on the gas as he dialed Leroux. The call was answered immediately.

"Tell me that was the cavalry I just heard go overhead."

"It was," confirmed Leroux. "Delta is inbound now. ETA ten minutes."

"Send me the coordinates."

"Negative, Colonel. I suggest you fall back to Cotabato City. This could get ugly."

His stomach boiled. "They're my people. My responsibility."

"Understood, Colonel. Good luck."

His phone vibrated in his hand.

MILF Controlled Village

Mindanao, The Philippines

"Nobody knows who we are or why we're here," whispered Bautista, translating the excited conversation nearby between their new captors.

"Doesn't surprise me," replied Acton. "I don't think we were taken by terrorists."

Laura's eyes narrowed. "Then who?"

"See what these guys are wearing on their feet? Shitty shoes, almost no boots, some are even barefoot. Did anyone notice what the guys were wearing that took us?"

Tommy's eyes bulged. "Boots. I noticed it when that guy stomped the phone."

"Exactly. *All* of them were wearing good quality boots."

Laura stared at him. "You're not suggesting—"

"That the Filipino government kidnapped us?"

"That's insane!" she hissed. "Why would they do that?"

Bautista shook his head. "It's not insane at all. Especially if they knew about the gold. I'm not saying that this is official. It's probably something rogue by some corrupt official with enough power to do this, but it's definitely not insane." He nodded toward the actual terrorists. "Their reaction certainly makes me think it's possible."

"Couldn't they have just stolen them?" suggested Mai. "I mean, their clothes certainly looked like these guys, and those balaclavas they had match the scarves these guys are wearing."

Acton shrugged. "Possible, but it doesn't explain why they didn't bring us into the village themselves. And it doesn't explain why these guys have no idea why we're here. If we were set up by some rogue element of the Philippines government, it explains everything."

Bautista lowered his head as one of the terrorists glanced in their direction. "I hate to end this discussion, but it doesn't really matter now. They're debating whether they should just kill us, or move us so we can be held for ransom."

"Maybe we should grease the wheels as you Americans say?"

Acton looked at his wife. "How? Tell them we're rich?"

"Exactly."

Bautista shook his head. "They won't believe you. Everybody probably says that, and they're suspicious. They think they're being set up, and it's better to just kill us. Forget the ransom."

"They won't forget it with the amount I can offer."

"They still won't believe you."

"Do they have the Internet here?"

Tommy shook his head. "I doubt it, unless they have some sort of satellite uplink, and I haven't seen any evidence of that. There's no way they're Googling us if that's what you're thinking."

"But they have radios, right?"

Acton nodded. "Yeah, I've seen a few walking around with them."

"Then they can call someone who does have the Internet."

Acton had to agree with his wife. At the moment, this seemed the only alternative. Offer a ridiculous payoff, with proof that they were good for it, rather than risk a beheading by suspicious terrorists notorious for just such things. He looked at the others. "What does everyone think? Should we tell them?"

Bautista's eyes widened. "It's too late. They've decided."

A machete was scraped on a large stone nearby, dark stains running down its sides suggesting tonight wouldn't be the first time it had tasted blood.

The Lotus

Tokyo, Japan

Takashi lay on the couch, each breath labored, each inhalation more painful than the last. His eyes were barely open, the ministrations of his "nurse" not noticed anymore.

"He's going to die."

Akira eyed the nurse. "Let him."

"The oyabun won't be happy if you break the agreement."

Akira backhanded the girl, sending her tumbling into Takashi, the pain excruciating. "Remember your place!"

The sobbing girl recovered, Takashi's pain relieved slightly, and she returned to gently stroking his hair. "I'm just trying to protect you," she sniffed.

"I don't need your protection. Someday I will be oyabun, and you will all swear your allegiance to me, and the softness shown by my father will be a thing of the past!" He stabbed a finger at Takashi. "Stop helping him."

"No."

Akira drew his weapon from its holster, aiming it at her. "I said stop helping him, or you're dead." He adjusted his aim, pointing it at Takashi instead. "Or maybe I'll just kill him. After all, I wouldn't want to lose my favorite whore over a disagreement."

She draped herself over Takashi, the pain unbearable. "I won't let you kill him."

Akira sighed, tipping the weapon toward the ceiling before holstering it. "Fine. Tend to a dead man. But I'll remember this the next time you ask me for a favor." He grabbed the phone. "Why haven't we heard from those idiots." He hit the speed dial for Hiroki and his eyes narrowed. "Who the hell is this?"

Mindanao, The Philippines

Leather ended the call. No matter how great the temptation, there was no time to have fun with the Japanese guy at the other end. He put the phone on vibrate in case what he assumed was the Yakuzas' master called back. According to his GPS, he was about twenty minutes from what might be the firefight of the year.

He checked his watch and cursed.

Delta was probably just arriving, and he was making such piss poor time, that he'd likely miss all the action, as well as the opportunity to protect his people.

A thunderous roar approaching from behind had him sticking his head out the window to catch a glimpse of what it might be, but again the trees blocked his view, though not his ears. What sounded like at least a dozen helicopters raced by, his finely tuned hearing suggesting old Hueys.

I'm guessing that's the Filipinos.

And it left him wondering why Delta had gone in ahead.

MILF Controlled Village

Mindanao, The Philippines

Dawson tossed the rope aside, his dangerous fast-roping drop complete. He rushed the tree line, the clearing selected for his team's insertion small though extremely close to the village. He would normally prefer to drop out of earshot of their targets, then hoof it in on foot, but the questionably motivated Filipinos were only ten minutes out, and the entire area was crawling with terrorists who could tip off their arrival regardless.

Speed was of the essence.

The chopper banked away and Dawson got his bearings. "Okay, gentlemen. Let's make this quick. The village is less than half a klick from here, they know we're coming, and we've got our *allies* ten minutes out. Let's have this wrapped up before they get there."

Niner came up beside him, his weapon trained on the jungle ahead as they advanced. "You really think we can't trust them?"

"I don't know. I just have a bad feeling. I don't think it's the troops themselves, it's whoever is commanding them. Those guys in the choppers are just following orders, but everything their commanders have been doing seems to be aimed at getting the hostages killed. None of the decisions made at the top have made any sense, and I have a funny feeling this isn't a rescue op at all."

Niner cursed. "Shit, BD, if you're suggesting what I think you're suggesting, we better put a wiggle on." He glanced back at the lumbering Atlas. "You better shake that money-maker, muscle boy, or you're going to be late."

"You just keep your eyes front, little man, otherwise you're liable to get clotheslined by some twig."

Dawson shook his head. "Let's keep it down. They know we're coming, but they don't need to know from where."

Acton struggled to keep his emotions in check as his head was pressed against the bloody stone. Two men held down his arms, and no matter how much he struggled, his executioner's foot on the middle of his back held him in place. He twisted his head to the side so he could see the others. If he died today, he was dying with his last images being of those he loved.

Laura was screaming at them, begging them to stop as tears streamed down her face, pleading with them that she'd pay anything they wanted. Bautista was terrified, translating her words to no avail as Tommy and Mai stood pressed against each other, Tommy staring at him, trying to be brave, Mai stealing glances, each time only managing to meet his gaze for moments before turning away.

It was never the way he pictured his end.

He had always imagined growing old, especially once Laura had entered his life. He wanted to live a long, full life, with her by his side, with his students becoming the men and women who would lead the world into a bright future.

He had wanted to see it all.

And he had never wanted the ones he loved to see him die so horribly, their final images of him his humiliating execution.

"Tell them we're rich!" screamed Laura. "Tell them we'll pay anything! Ten million! A hundred million! I don't care! Just tell them! For the love of God, tell them!"

Bautista continued his pleas then fell silent as the executioner raised his machete high over his head.

They all fell silent.

"I love you!" he shouted. "I love you all!"

Laura dropped to her knees. "I love you too!"

"Don't look. Whatever you do, don't watch me die. Please!"

"I have to."

"I don't want to be remembered like this."

Tommy turned away, Mai's head pressed into his chest, and Laura's shoulders slumped as she closed her eyes, her entire body shaking with her sobs.

And his executioner inhaled, the foot pressed into his back increasing its pressure.

"Goodbye."

Somebody shouted and he heard something in the distance.

Is that a helicopter?

His right hand was released, the grip on the left loosened slightly, and the foot pressing him into the stone eased up.

You're not dying without a fight.

He yanked his left hand free as he rolled to his right. His executioner lost his balance as Acton leaped to his feet and sprinted toward two huts only feet away. He ran between them and into the jungle, gunfire erupting behind him as Laura screamed for him to run. Bullets slammed into tree trunks around him and he ducked, folding in his arms as tightly as he could, providing the smallest target possible as he continued to flee. He cut to the left, placing one of the huts between him and the gunmen, then rushed forward as fast as he could, thanking God his hands had been freed in preparation for the liberation of his head from his neck.

Shouts behind him and the sounds of his pursuers reaching the trees had his mind racing as he tried to plan his escape on the fly. Moments ago death was certain, and now he had to make sure it wasn't a short reprieve.

And every loud crash he made as he pushed through the underbrush, every snapped tree limb, gave away his position. He spotted a large tree ahead and made a beeline for it. He pressed into the large roots on the opposite side, struggling to control his breathing as his pursuers approached, their shouts providing him with some cover.

They rushed past him without slowing down, and he was about to stand when he felt something. He looked down and gasped as a large centipede crawled down his shoulder and across his chest. He held his breath, his heart slamming from a mix of terror, disgust, and physical exertion, then leaped to his feet the moment it crawled back onto the tree trunk.

"Stop."

The voice behind him sounded young. Terrified. Unsure.

He raised his hands and turned to find a young man, perhaps in his late teens, pointing an AK-47 at him, the barrel shaking dramatically as uncontrolled adrenaline overwhelmed the gunman.

Acton waited for it to swing slightly to the right then darted forward, shoving the barrel aside and delivering a punch to the man's nose with the heel of his hand. He collapsed to his knees, blood pouring from his nose as Acton tore the weapon from his hands, driving the butt into the top of his head, rendering him unconscious.

Sorry, kid.

He ejected the magazine and cursed, finding it empty. He quickly searched the boy and found nothing on him but a good-sized knife.

He sighed, rolling his eyes at the heavens.

Really?

Niner raised a fist and pointed ahead at the sound of approaching hostiles, if their shouting was any indication. Dawson could order them taken out, but in these close quarters with trees in the way, the likelihood of eliminating what sounded like at least half a dozen before one of them could get a shot off, was unlikely.

And he had a feeling those approaching weren't there for them.

He signaled for the team to take cover, then pressed his back against a large tree as the loud rush of flesh neared then passed, continuing away from their destination.

Dawson emerged from his cover. "Niner, you and Atlas watch our sixes."

"Roger that," replied Niner, taking a position behind one of the trees, facing the enemy that had just passed.

Dawson activated his comms. "Control, Zero-One. ETA on our friends, over?"

"Four minutes."

"Copy that." He pressed forward. "Let's move. This is going to be tight."

Acton heard something ahead and to his right. His immediate thought was that the men who had charged past him were returning. But they were too quiet.

An animal?

He headed away from the sound, to his left, and farther from the village, still uncertain as to what he could do with just a hunting knife. If he could get the jump on one of the others, one with an actual weapon with ammo, he at least stood a fighting chance.

There were at least twenty armed guys in the village. Who are you kidding?

Yet he had to do something. Laura and the kids were still being held, and their time might be limited.

His eyes widened as a forgotten thought returned.

The helicopter!

He was certain he had heard a helicopter. It was what had distracted everybody. Could the Filipinos be staging a rescue? Could Kane's people be arriving?

A surge of renewed hope rushed through him as he continued to cut away from the sound he had heard.

Then he froze.

Ahead of him, toward the right, he could see a figure hiding behind a tree, a weapon pointed at the jungle, away from the village. That meant it had to be one of the terrorists, positioned to repel whoever had just arrived in the helicopter.

He had to stop him.

He crept forward, his knife at the ready, placing each foot as carefully as he could. He was bringing a knife to a gunfight, and a single snapping twig could give away his position and this would all be over. But ahead of him wasn't just the enemy, it was a gun he could possibly use to save Laura and the others.

He was feet away now, then inches.

He pressed the knife against the back of the man's neck. "Now, why don't you drop that weapon."

Something pressed against his back and he cursed.

An impossibly deep voice rumbled behind him. "Why don't you drop yours?"

His eyes shot wide. "Atlas?"

His target turned his head. "Doc?"

Acton's eyes bulged. "Niner?"

Atlas grabbed him by the shoulder, spinning him around. "Doc?"

Acton's shoulders collapsed in relief, every muscle, tensed to the extreme, relaxing. "Oh, thank God you're here." He pointed toward the village. "They have Laura and the others. We have to hurry. They were about to chop off my favorite body part when they heard your helicopter."

Niner tapped Acton's junk with the muzzle of his MP5. "Good thing we got here when we did."

Acton gave him a look then tapped his head. "I was talking about my head, you moron."

Niner grinned. "So was I." He activated his comm. "Zero-One, One-One. We've got the Doc, over."

Laura shook her shoulders, struggling to rid herself of the foot pressed against her back, yet it was futile. The man was simply too strong, and with her hands still bound behind her back, she couldn't gain any leverage. Tommy and Mai were screaming, begging the man with the machete to stop, but Laura had long ago given up.

There was no reasoning with these people.

At least James will live.

Her eyes burned as she thought of him, alone, forced to carry on without her, and the guilt he would feel for having run. Yet he had no choice, and not for a moment did she think he had abandoned them, and not for a moment did she not think he was doing everything he could to try and help them.

But he was alone, unarmed, against dozens.

Her eyes met Mai's and she mouthed the words she had lost the voice to utter.

I love you both!

Mai struggled to break free of the man holding her as she screamed at them. He jabbed the butt of his rifle into her stomach, sending her to her knees.

"You bastard!" Tommy booted the man in the groin, doubling him over, and Tommy's captor punched him in the face, sending him tumbling into Mai.

Laura found her voice. "Don't fight them! You'll just make it worse for yourselves!"

Tommy struggled to his knees, Mai at his side, and they both just stared at her, resigned to their fate.

"Close your eyes! And please forgive me for bringing you here."

"It's not your fault," said Tommy, his shoulders shaking as he struggled to breathe.

"Close your eyes!"

They did, and she closed hers as the machete rose into the night sky.

Then clattered to the ground.

She opened her eyes and twisted her head to see her executioner gripping his chest, blood rapidly flowing down his stomach as he crumpled to his knees. She turned toward Tommy and Mai and her jaw dropped as both the men holding them collapsed, followed by the man holding Bautista.

Gunfire erupted.

She rolled off the rock then hugged it, using it as cover. "Get down!"

She couldn't see Tommy and Mai from her vantage point. She struggled to inch forward to get an eye on them, her bonds making it difficult. Gunfire slammed into the rock, halting her advance as she dropped her head into the dirt, her captors eager to finish the job they had started before whoever was coming to their rescue could succeed.

And her only thoughts were for the kids.

"Keep down!"

Dawson pressed forward, picking off targets in his arc as Spock did the same to his right. He made certain to use the huts as cover as their panicked enemy fired randomly into the night, not yet having acquired them. Jimmy and Jagger were sweeping one side of the village as he and Spock did the other, with Niner and Atlas still covering their six.

Laura was huddled behind the stone at the center of the village, her executioner he had taken out only moments before bleeding onto the dirt beside her. Tommy and Mai hugged the ground along with Bautista, and all appeared alive for the moment.

"Eleven o'clock!" barked Spock and Dawson adjusted slightly, removing one of their opponents as the man turned his weapon toward the hostages.

He dropped.

And Spock cried out.

Dawson didn't take his eyes off his arc, the cry more of a stubbed-toe yelp. "You good?"

"Caught one in the right leg. Just a scratch. I'm good."

Dawson breathed a sigh of relief as he took out his next target, still advancing toward the hostages. "Glad to hear it. Might I suggest you move a little to the left next time?"

"I will if you tell me it's coming."

Dawson chuckled as he fired another round. "Reloading." He ejected his mag and slapped another in its place.

"Zero-One, Control Actual. Those choppers are about to be right on top of you."

"Copy that. Gentlemen, we've got seconds before a possible shitstorm."

Philippine Army National Headquarters
Fort Bonifacio, Manila, The Philippines

Ocampo was pacing now, the pressure simply too much. The Americans had been on the ground for almost ten minutes now, and he had no idea what was going on. Had the hostages been rescued? Had they told them of the gold? Were they about to be exposed for what they had done?

Were they about to be arrested and sent to prison?

He couldn't see a way out of it now, their original plan shot to hell the moment the Americans left their inferior helicopters behind.

"Tell them to light up the area. Put everything they've got on that encampment. That's an order." Cruz moved the microphone of his headset away from his mouth as his cousin stared at him, wide-eyed.

"Are you insane? You're going to kill the Americans."

Cruz shrugged. "They broke formation."

"But if we kill Americans, we'll never get away with it!"

Cruz glared at him. "You fool! Don't you realize what is happening here? If the Americans rescue the hostages, they'll tell them about the gold, then the secret is out. We were supposed to arrive at the same time. We were supposed to tell them our contact had told us the hostages were dead, then we were supposed to lay waste to the area, with or without the Americans' agreement. There'd be no witnesses to the kidnapping, and nobody to tell anyone about the gold."

"But the Americans are already there. If they rescued the hostages, then they might have already told them about the gold."

"Which is why they all have to die." Cruz folded his arms. "Remember what you said? We have to stop thinking like regular people. Once we have the gold, we can pay off anyone we need to, and disappear anywhere in the world. We'll be untouchable."

Ocampo sighed, shaking his head. "I hope you're right."

"I know I am."

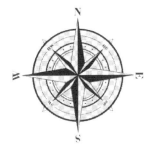

MILF Controlled Village

Mindanao, The Philippines

The guns fell silent.

Laura lay frozen on the ground, the stone that was to be the site of her final breath having protected her through the brutal attack. She rolled over and struggled to her feet when she saw a shadow emerge from the darkness, the large knife in his hand the only thing her eyes could focus on.

She squeezed them shut as her arm was grabbed, the knife plunging toward her.

Then her hands were free.

"You okay, Professor?"

It was a voice she would recognize anywhere. She was hauled to her feet and she embraced her savior. "BD!" she cried, her shoulders shaking as he pushed her away.

"We're not secure yet, and we have to bug out in less than thirty seconds." He slapped the knife in her hand and pointed at the others. "Cut them loose and stay down."

She nodded and he pressed forward as she scurried over to the others. She cut Mai free then Tommy. Mai grabbed Laura in a bearhug. Laura held the knife out for Tommy, motioning with her eyes toward Bautista. Tommy cut him free as Mai sobbed.

"Laura!"

She spun at the sound of James' voice to see him at the tree line, beckoning them. Without a word, she grabbed Tommy and Mai by an arm and rose, racing for the trees. Gunfire erupted just behind them and lead tore into the dirt at their feet. She pulled everyone down to the ground and gasped when two shadows in the jungle took form as they surged forward, muzzle flashes erupting from their weapons as Niner and Atlas eliminated a survivor emerging from one of the huts.

The two operators continued past them, their weapons sweeping the area for other targets. She looked up to see James rushing forward, his hand extended. She took it and he hauled her to her feet, then they both grabbed the others and continued to the trees.

Suddenly the hut behind them erupted into a fireball as the thunder of choppers and rocket fire overwhelmed the area.

Operations Center 2, CIA Headquarters

Langley, Virginia

Child's hands were in the air, his mouth agape. "What the hell do they think they're doing?"

Leroux shook his head as he rushed toward the display, his heart pounding at the satellite images showing a dozen Filipino helicopters emptying their weapons pods on the small village holding the hostages and their Delta team.

"Don't they know our people are in there?" cried Tong. "Not to mention the hostages?"

Leroux shook his head as he exchanged a shocked look with his boss, Director Morrison. "They don't care!"

Morrison agreed. "No, they don't. You were right. This is a rogue op."

Dawson's voice came in over the comms. "Control, Zero-One! We're taking heavy fire here! Request assistance! Over!"

Leroux activated his comm. "Stand by, Zero-One." He turned to Morrison. "We need that contingency."

Morrison tapped his phone, pressing it to his ear. "Requesting Omega Package." He ended the call. "Done."

MILF Controlled Village

Mindanao, The Philippines

Dawson cursed as another hut erupted in a fireball. He activated his comm. "Confirm the hostages are secure?"

"Affirmative!" replied Niner. "Let's get the hell out of here!"

"Roger that. Everyone fall back to the exfil point!"

Dawson sprinted toward the trees, Spock on his heels, ignoring the explosions around him and the rockets raining down on them. There was no point. If one of them had his name on it, it was meant to be, and every second he wasted ducking or weaving was another second in the line of fire.

Women and children screamed, forgotten in the mayhem the fact this was a village, not a military base.

There were innocent people here.

Yet they weren't his problem. His mission was to save the professors and their team, along with his men. It was up to the Filipinos to protect these villagers, and they weren't doing a hell of a good job of it.

I guess you were right.

His gut had told him something was wrong, and the fact they were fired upon by their so-called allies confirmed it. Though he wasn't sure he could blame the men above him. From everything he had seen with this op, he was certain it was someone at the top pulling the strings. He wouldn't be surprised if the men in the choppers had no clue about the hostages, and no clue he and his team were in the line of fire.

This was a search and destroy mission.

They were probably told this was a MILF encampment, and they were sent in to eliminate it. And the safest way to do that was from the air.

He reached the trees and dove into the cover they provided, the village behind them the focus of the weapons bombarding the area.

When I find out who's behind this, I'm taking them out.

Acton firmly gripped Laura's hand as they followed Niner and Atlas through the jungle. Explosions tore apart the village behind them as heavy gunfire from .50 caliber pintle-mounted door guns belched lead on the innocent and guilty below.

Their escape had been narrow, and he was concerned whether the rest of Bravo Team had made it out in time. They were with Niner and Atlas, but there were twelve members of the team he had met over the years, though rarely were they all involved in any one mission.

Niner raised a fist, bringing them to a halt. He signaled for everyone to take a knee, then pointed slightly to their right. Acton cocked an ear as he dropped with the others, the distinctive sounds of people crashing through the jungle growing.

"Could be the guys that came after me," whispered Acton.

Niner agreed. "Could be." He handed his Glock over along with two mags, Atlas doing the same with Laura. "Try not to shoot any friendlies."

Acton held the gun by the barrel. "Which end do I point?"

"Funny." Niner gestured left then right. "Spread out, watch your arcs, and don't shoot until I give the order."

"Or me if the little man gets hit," said Atlas.

"With the size of target you offer, I find that unlikely."

Acton pointed to a large tree and turned to Tommy, Mai, and Bautista. "Keep behind that and out of the line of fire." They nodded, all hurrying out of sight, and Acton headed left with Niner, Laura right with Atlas, all weapons trained toward the sounds.

The first crashed through the trees and into sight. Acton's finger moved to the trigger, yet he resisted the urge to fire, waiting for Niner or Atlas to give the order. More emerged, and he understood why they were waiting.

Get everyone visible.

About half a dozen had pursued him, and he was certain Bravo Team was well-aware of the count.

And he counted six.

"Now!"

He took aim, firing directly ahead then to his right as Niner did the same and to the left. He spotted Atlas and Laura's position open fire, and within moments, all six terrorists were down, not a single shot fired in opposition.

"Gotta love the element of surprise," boomed Atlas

Acton rose after Niner did. "Why do I feel kind of bad about this?"

Niner glanced at him. "Because this village had nothing to do with what's happened today. But don't feel too bad, Doc, these guys weren't looking to give you all a haircut with that machete. These are bad people."

Acton rubbed his neck. "Good point. I kind of like my head where it is."

Dawson rounded the village as it was bombarded from above, his weapon raised in the event they encountered a fleeing hostile. Spock was at his side when a heavy burst of MP5 and Glock gunfire erupted at his 10 o'clock.

"Something's up," said Spock as they adjusted their heading.

"No return fire that I heard."

"Me neither."

The sound of a missile streaking overhead then a near-immediate explosion as it found its target had him hitting the ground.

"Bravo Team, take cover!"

"Everyone down!" ordered Niner, but nobody needed to be told, the missiles overhead slamming into their targets enough impetus to have everyone diving for cover. Acton rolled to see the flaming fuselages of several helicopters dropping out of the sky.

"What the hell is going on?"

Niner rose to his feet and hauled Acton to his. "Backup plan. Let's move before one of those helicopters decides to drop on us!"

Acton pulled Laura to her feet as a helicopter beat a hasty retreat overhead.

Dawson held up a fist bringing Spock to a halt beside him. He pointed ahead, the sound of people approaching having them both raising their weapons slightly.

But only slightly.

This was about where he expected Niner and Atlas to be with the rescued hostages, and he wasn't about to empty a mag into a bunch of friendlies, despite the chaos overhead raising his adrenaline a notch.

The sounds stopped.

"Disco!"

Spock chuckled and Dawson shook his head at Niner's challenge.

"Thunder," he replied.

Niner emerged from the trees, spinning his arms and pivoting his hips, executing a remarkably good Travolta imitation. "Disco thunder, baby!"

Atlas rolled his eyes as he led the hostages from the thick foliage. "If a helicopter doesn't drop on his head, request permission to put him out of our misery."

Spock cocked an eyebrow as he glanced up at another exploding helicopter. "If your moves are hot enough, one of those AMRAAMs are liable to lock onto you."

Dawson chuckled as he turned, leading the way to their exfil point. Plan B had been implemented, the F/A-18E Super Hornets, on standby the moment the mission had begun, unleashing their AIM-120 Advanced Medium-Range Air-to-Air Missiles from outside the Philippines' territorial waters, and at over 3,000mph, reaching their targets in under two minutes.

The poor bastards didn't have a chance.

He felt for them, as he was fairly certain they thought they were firing on a terrorist base. Yet he couldn't allow his men and their targets to be injured or killed because of corruption up the chain of command.

And if that wasn't the reason, then he had no sympathy at all, for it meant they were knowingly firing on his friends.

The din of battle faded, the remaining choppers bugging out, the only sounds now the carnage left behind of roaring fires and wailing innocents.

He activated his comm. "Control, Zero-One. We're clear. ETA at LZ two minutes."

Operations Center 2, CIA Headquarters

Langley, Virginia

"The rest are turning tail."

Leroux watched the satellite images overlaid with data from the AWACS in the area monitoring the battle. The AMRAAMs had done their job, taking out four of the hostiles, the rest getting the message in short order.

They weren't his concern anymore.

He watched the Sea Hawk approach the exfil point, the Delta team's locators showing them nearly in position. This op was almost over, and at the moment appeared successful.

Yet things weren't over.

Not by a long shot.

He turned to his team as the door opened and Director Morrison entered. "I want everything we have on this Vice Commander. If he's not behind this, then he knows who is. I want to know who's responsible for this Charlie-Foxtrot."

Morrison eyed the screen for a moment. "This is going to get ugly. A lot of Filipino soldiers died today."

Leroux nodded. "Blame their commander."

"Agreed. Let me know what you find. We may have to pay him a visit."

Leroux chuckled. "I think you'll have a few volunteers from Bravo Team if you're looking."

Morrison smiled. "I have no doubt." He headed for the door. "I have a feeling I'll be in meetings for the foreseeable future, dealing with the international incident we just created. Get me some intel. It would be nice to have a finger to point at other than ourselves."

Mindanao, The Philippines

Leather cursed at the fireballs ahead. He couldn't make out what was going on through the dense foliage, though he was fairly certain he had heard missiles inbound only moments before.

Something must have gone horribly wrong.

If Delta had arrived first, there would have been a firefight, perhaps some minor detonations, even more significant secondary explosions if a munitions cache was hit.

But missiles? Major explosions moments later?

And what was the target? The village? What else was there to target?

His eyes bulged.

The Filipino helicopters!

He had heard them go overhead a full ten minutes after the Black Hawk. Could they be the target? And why had Delta gone in so far ahead?

He shook his head. Something was going on here, something that couldn't be part of the plan.

The sound of a Black Hawk passing overhead had him pressing on the accelerator, road conditions and potential roadblocks be damned. Anybody manning them would be heading toward the battle, and if he killed his vehicle, so be it.

He had to get aboard that chopper.

The Sea Hawk bounced and the crew waved them forward. Dawson guided their freed hostages toward the chopper and the crew helped them on board as flames and secondary explosions continued to color the sky less than a mile away.

Washington must be going apeshit.

He couldn't wait to read the report on this one. He just hoped whoever was behind it was brought to justice. He'd hate to waste precious leave taking care of it himself.

Don't mess with my men, my family, my friends.

Or my country.

"BD! Six o'clock!"

Dawson swung toward Niner's warning and raised his weapon at the vehicle racing toward them. "Prepare to engage!"

His team spread out to protect the civilians and the chopper, when the truck skidded to a halt and the door flew open.

"It's me! Cameron Leather! Hold your fire!"

Dawson lowered his weapon, signaling the others to do the same. "Just in the nick of time, Colonel."

Leather chuckled as he strode over to join them. "I guess I missed all the excitement."

Dawson pointed to the chopper. "Get on board. This place will be filthy with MILF soon."

Niner snickered as he climbed inside the chopper, Tommy as well, and as the helicopter rose, they were all laughing, the tension of the situation getting the better of their sense of decorum.

Dawson stared out the window at the village below, and said a silent prayer for the innocent, for innocent lives were definitely lost today.

"Where are you taking us?" asked Acton.

"USS Ronald Reagan."

Acton shook his head. "No, we have to go back to the cave."

"Why?"

"We need to secure the gold."

Niner's eyes widened. "Is it real?"

"Yes."

"How much?"

"Enough to fill Fort Knox."

Niner's eyes were saucers. "Really?"

Acton laughed. "No, but it's a hell of a damned lot, let me tell you."

Philippine Army National Headquarters

Fort Bonifacio, Manila, The Philippines

The room was in a panic, including Ocampo, for if what he was overhearing was true, the unthinkable had just happened, and they were doomed.

He grabbed his cousin by the arm. "What's going on?"

Cruz yanked his arm free. "They're firing on our helicopters!"

"Who?"

"The Americans! They launched from outside our airspace." He threw his headset across the room. "How dare they!"

Ocampo pulled at his hair as he stared up at the ceiling. "I told you firing on them was stupid! What are we going to do now?"

Cruz growled, leaning on his desk, his fists clenched, his knuckles turning white. "We have to secure the gold. This is still our country. We don't owe them any explanations."

"But we fired on their position."

Cruz stood. "No. We'll say we didn't know they were there because they broke formation. We took fire from the ground and returned fire. It's our word against theirs. Nobody trusts the Americans. We'll be fine."

Ocampo's eyebrows rose at the statement. "I'm not so sure about that nobody thing." His eyes widened. "And what are you going to tell the President?"

Cruz squared his shoulders. "That under the authority granted me by my position, I had our troops execute a joint operation with the Americans to rescue a group of foreigners that had been taken hostage by extremists." He exhaled loudly. "I'll probably lose my job, but with the amount of money we're about to have, they'll never find me." He dropped into his chair. "Do you have the convoy ready?"

Ocampo nodded. "Yes. I've had the airport rent a dozen trucks. I'm using men I trust to drive them. I sent them the moment we saw those Americanos on the drone footage. They'll be there in the morning. I'm flying out—" He paused as he spotted something at the far end of the large room.

His cousin noticed it too.

Military police.

"Get out of here, now!" hissed Cruz. "Get the gold, then pay off whoever you need to get me out."

Ocampo grabbed his cousin by the shoulder. "You can count on me."

Cruz pointed to a door at the opposite end. "That door, end of the hall, down the stairs and take the emergency exit. You'll be fine. They're here for me."

Ocampo headed for the door at as casual a pace as he dared, the shouts of surprise at the police charging into the secure area getting louder. He opened the door and stepped into the hall, closing it behind him, relieved to find only regular personnel. He walked briskly now, not a second to lose, and as he stepped outside, a smile spread.

If you think I'm spending a penny on getting you out of prison, Cousin, you're in for one hell of a surprise.

Operations Center 2, CIA Headquarters

Langley, Virginia

Leroux glanced over his shoulder as the door to the operations center beeped then hissed open. Director Morrison entered looking as haggard as he felt.

"What's the word, sir?"

"They just arrested the Vice Commander based on your intel. Apparently, the Philippines' President was surprised to find out about our joint operation. Turns out he didn't authorize it."

"Surprise, surprise."

Morrison nodded. "I should never doubt your gut."

"Well, we still would have participated, I'm guessing, just going in with our eyes wide open." Leroux motioned toward the displays, the feeds from several body cameras showing everyone happy and healthy in the Sea Hawk. "The extraction went well. We have all the hostages unharmed, and Colonel Leather managed to reach them on time for the evac."

"Excellent." Morrison turned toward the team. "Good work, people. You saved lives today. Now we just need to figure out what caused the Vice Commander of the Philippines Army to go rogue."

Child raised a hand. "Umm, I might have something on that."

Leroux turned to him. "What?"

"Well, we've been figuring it has to do with the gold, obviously, but we couldn't figure out how he would have found out." He gestured toward the display as a file was brought up on a Colonel Ramil Ocampo. "This is the general's cousin, Colonel Ocampo. He's the head of security at the Ninoy Aquino International Airport. If you recall, Leather reported Yakuza at the cave site. We found that five arrived at the airport, and one was arrested for shooting a guard. Obviously, the Yakuza knew about the gold, which means so did the one that was arrested. The cousin finds out during the interrogation, goes to his cousin with the military assets capable of recovering it, then they hatch a plan to deceive us."

Morrison folded his arms and squeezed his chin. "But how did they know about the professors?"

"They came through the same airport a few hours later, so it's possible."

Leroux shook his head. "Unlikely. There's no way they could have made the connection. My guess is the cousin finds out about the gold from his Yakuza prisoner, tells the Vice Commander, who sends the drone Leather reported to make sure the coast is clear. They find the professors there, so then send in a team, posing as terrorists, to kidnap them."

Child interrupted. "Why not just kill them? It wouldn't be that out of the ordinary there."

"Because it *would* be out of the ordinary. The Philippines is violent, but outside of terrorist activity, rarely are half a dozen tourists or academics murdered in cold blood. Hostage taking, however, is very common, especially in Mindanao. Kill them outright, questions get raised, people come to investigate, and your gold recovery operation is discovered. Kidnap them, make everyone think terrorists did it, call in the US military to help you rescue them, then kill them accidentally in the process, and no one ever thinks to ask where they were when they were taken."

Morrison sat in one of the free chairs. "If it weren't for Colonel Leather, we never would have known."

Leroux sat across from him. "If it weren't for Agent Kane's quick thinking, Leather would have been captured with the rest of them, and we wouldn't have known half of what we did."

"And thanks to his suspicions, your gut, and one Delta Command Sergeant Major's experience, we know something is up, Delta goes in ahead of the joint team, and screws up their plans to fake taking fire and level the village, killing all the witnesses to the fact the gold had been found."

"Exactly. They panicked. They were afraid that the hostages would tell Delta what they had found, and they couldn't have it. They fired the moment they were within range."

"Bastards," muttered Child.

"I still wonder how much the guys in the air knew. I think they thought they were firing on a terrorist stronghold, not hostages and American soldiers."

"Well, they might have figured it out when a few AMRAAMs were shoved up their asses."

Tong snorted. "They definitely messed with the wrong people."

Child raised a finger. "Umm, sirs, I just got a report that the helicopter is deviating from its planned flightpath."

Leroux rose. "What? Where are they headed?"

"It looks like their new course will take them directly to the gold."

Maliit na Bahay, Mindanao, The Philippines

"Fire in the hole!"

Everyone ducked behind the ridgeline as Niner pressed the detonator. The explosion shook the ground, sending debris raining down across the clearing in front of the cave, a cloud of dust rolling toward them that took several minutes for the breeze to clear.

"Everyone stay put!" ordered Niner as he rose and jogged over to the detonation site to confirm all the explosives had gone off. "All clear!"

Acton rose along with the others and smiled as the cave entrance came into sight. A large hole was now visible, wide enough to walk through upright, though there were still a lot of rocks underfoot to be wary of. He turned to Bautista.

"Buwan, this is your discovery. Would you do us the honor of showing our friends what this is all about?"

Bautista grinned. "With pleasure!" He led the Bravo Team inside the cave, flashlights flicking on as each of them entered, dawn just cracking the horizon outside. He gestured toward the remains. "These were the villagers from the settlement down the hill. According to the lone survivor, they were used as manual labor to haul what you are about to see up the hill from the trucks that brought it here. Once they were finished, they were sealed inside, and likely died from lack of water after several agonizing days."

"And the guy who did this is still alive?" asked Niner.

"Yes."

Atlas growled. "I'd like to pay him a visit."

"Me too," agreed Niner.

Bautista continued deeper into the cave. "When the dust settles from this, I'll be making a full report to my government. They will probably want the Japanese government to arrest the man so he can be tried for war crimes."

"He'd have to be around a hundred years old," said Acton. "He'd probably die from the stress of the trial."

"Good!" echoed most of those around him, and he had to agree. No matter how much guilt the man hopefully suffered over the years, this was a crime that couldn't go unpunished, even if in the end it was purely symbolic. These people needed justice, and needed to be remembered. And if it took trying a 100-year-old man, then so be it. He had no sympathy for him.

I was just following orders.

He shook his head. Whoever did this had options. He could have executed his orders, then informed the Filipinos quietly where they were so they could be rescued in time. Instead, he made a choice to massacre hundreds.

All for gold and the glory of the Empire.

And, with the amount of gold they were now looking at, giving that Empire the means from which to rebuild so they could live to fight another day.

Killing more innocents.

"Holy shit!" exclaimed Niner as he picked up one of the gold bars. "This is heavy." He tossed it to Atlas who easily caught it and executed several bicep curls.

"Hey, BD, can I keep a few? They'd look great in my weight room."

Dawson chuckled. "I'll see what we can arrange." He turned to Bautista. "Any idea how much there is?"

"No, we never got a chance to properly catalog it. It will take weeks if not months to properly deal with the site. First, we have to deal with the bodies. We can't desecrate this place moving gold through their bones."

"We're talking billions?"

"Absolutely. Tens if not hundreds."

Niner cursed, turning to Acton. "Are you sure it wouldn't fill Fort Knox?"

Acton shrugged. "I'd be willing to try."

Dawson ended the tour with a check of his watch. "We have to leave. Being off-mission for a few minutes is fine, but we're overdue."

"We can't leave this unguarded. Too many know where it is now."

Dawson shook his head as he headed out of the cave, his team following. "Sorry, Doc, I've got my orders. And besides, the Vice Commander who was behind this has been arrested. Your gold is probably safe for the next few days at least."

Bautista stopped at the mouth of the cave. "I'm staying."

Dawson regarded him. "You're a Filipino citizen. It's your right to do so, though I wouldn't recommend it."

"I'm staying too," said Acton. "They arrested the Vice Commander, but didn't you say his cousin was involved too? Does anybody know where he is?"

Dawson sighed. "Listen, Doc. A lot of people are dead because of what happened. I'm not about to just leave you here to have to do it all again."

"Not to mention I could have died." Spock pointed at the tiny scrape on his leg. "A few inches to the left and my best friend could have been decapitated."

Dawson headed toward the Sea Hawk idling nearby then stopped, pressing his earpiece. "Copy that, Control." He turned to the others. "We've got a convoy of trucks heading this way. They'll be here in fifteen minutes. And we've got a chopper that's inbound, originating in Manila."

Niner frowned. "Well, if you were wondering where that missing cousin is, I'd bet he's probably on board."

"I'm not willing to take that bet. He commands hundreds of troops. Those trucks could be fully loaded with them." He pointed at the helicopter. "Everyone on board, now!"

Bautista folded his arms, defiant. "No! We can't let this get looted. I'm staying. You have no authority over me. I've devoted most of my life to finding this, and the memory of an entire village is at stake. These people died to preserve this secret, and I owe it to Juan to make sure the world knows of their sacrifice."

Leather turned to him. "They'll kill you, and the secret will die with you. You can't stop them. We have to go." He turned to Laura. "Please, ma'am, listen to the sergeant major. We have to get out of here."

Tommy cleared his throat. "Umm, I've got an idea."

Everyone turned to him. "What?" asked an impatient Dawson.

"Can I talk to Mr. Leroux?"

Dawson activated his comm. "Control Actual, Zero-One. Stand by for Thomas Granger, over." He handed his comm gear to Tommy who then walked away, a rapid-fire conversation between two geeks underway. Dawson turned to the others. "I don't know what that kid thinks he's got cooking, but we're leaving. We're not supposed to be here. A US military chopper and half a dozen Spec Ops soldiers on Philippines territory is going to cause even more problems, especially after we shot a few of their choppers out of the sky a couple of hours ago."

Acton had to acknowledge that Dawson was right, but so was Bautista. There was no denying they didn't stand a chance against perhaps hundreds of troops. Yet would they kill them now that they knew the US government was aware who they were and where they were? And were likely watching with a drone or satellite? They might just be arrested.

Not with that much gold.

His heart sank. This was the Philippines government they were dealing with. This was a corrupt colonel, whose corrupt cousin just tried to kill them, all under the watchful eyes of these brave men who had rescued them. These new arrivals didn't care about the law, didn't care about who knew. There was enough gold in that cave to get away with anything, including murder, then disappear forever.

They had to leave with Dawson.

"We can do it!" announced Tommy, returning with the comm gear which he held up. "But I need this to do it."

"Do what?" asked Dawson.

"Make it so that they don't dare touch us, or steal the gold."

"How?"

Niner interrupted. "BD, we've just been ordered out. Now. With or without them."

Dawson acknowledged the order. "Okay, we're out of here. Are you people coming with us?"

Acton regarded Tommy. "Are you sure?"

"I think so. Leroux thinks it could work too."

Acton turned to Laura who nodded slightly. "We have to try," she said.

And he agreed. He extended a hand to Dawson. "We're staying. If things go sideways, don't risk your lives to come get us. This was our choice."

Dawson shook his hand. "I hope you know what you're doing, Doc."

Acton grunted. "So do I." He watched as Dawson and the others boarded the chopper, the massive Sea Hawk lifting off moments later and disappearing from view, its thundering rotors fading in the distance. He turned to Tommy. "I really hope you have a plan."

Tommy nodded, fear on his face as he realized this was all on him if it failed. "I do." He tapped the communications gear. "Now, who wants to talk to the world?"

"Huh?"

Approaching Maliit na Bahay, Mindanao, The Philippines

"ETA?"

"Five minutes," replied Ocampo's pilot, Captain Salazar. "The convoy has just arrived."

Ocampo smiled. "Excellent. I want you to put me directly in front of that cave if you can. I need to be the first inside."

"I'll have to see if the area is big enough, but I'll try." Salazar glanced at Ocampo. "What's this all about, sir? Normally, I just ferry VIPs from the airport. I've never flown anyone this far before. Certainly not to the middle of nowhere in Mindanao."

"I needed someone I could trust." Ocampo stared at him. "Can I trust you, Captain?"

Salazar's eyes widened. "Of course, sir!"

"Good. Once we get there, you'll understand what this is all about, and you'll be able to write your own ticket. You'll have any posting you want, and a promotion."

Salazar smiled. "Major Salazar. I like the sound of that."

"Maybe one day it'll be colonel. Or general." Ocampo thought of his cousin, and whether he was suffering the same indignities a prisoner of his own might. He doubted they'd beat him. Not somebody so high profile. But his life as he knew it was certainly over.

Serves him right.

The bastard had always treated him like dirt, despite being a year younger than him. At family gatherings, Ocampo was the one who should be treated with more respect than the younger Cruz, and it was once true, the familial hierarchy intact.

Then Cruz became a general, then the Vice Commander. He had fulfilled his family obligations by securing the job as head of security at the airport for him, and in doing so, the family dynamic had changed.

Cruz was the most respected.

And he could say nothing about it, otherwise he'd lose his job.

He had to grin and bear it at every gathering, suppress the anger every time his wife mentioned his cousin's name and how they owed him so much.

It was all true.

And it all drove him nuts.

He smiled as he imagined the next family gathering, where Cruz would be in prison, and the lowly colonel would be handing out gold bars to everyone.

That gold better be there.

Operations Center 2, CIA Headquarters

Langley, Virginia

"Do you have it?"

Child nodded at Leroux then pointed at the main display, a shaky video feed appearing. Leroux activated his comm, responding to Tommy.

"We've got it."

"And the upload?"

A thumbs up from Child.

"Affirmative."

"Good, that has the footage from inside. I suggest some sort of split-screen. My broadcast alongside the footage on a loop. Feel free to clean it up for content."

"I'm on it!" said Child, his video editing skills put to the test, his efforts shown on another screen as footage taken from inside the cave showing the bodies and the treasure were stitched together for what was to be a Hail Mary pass.

One that if unsuccessful, could mean the deaths of half a dozen innocent people.

On camera.

"How's the image?" asked Tommy, the camera now stable and focused on Professor Bautista. "The sun is just coming up. I don't want it to screw with the camera."

"Everything looks great at this end. Nice and clear. Just try to keep things steady."

"Will do. How's viewership?"

Leroux glanced at the counter showing a trickle of Tommy's podcast followers taking notice of his live feed. "Next to nil, but we just kicked in the bots, and the link is being disseminated to every media organization in the world as we speak. Our bots will have this trending on social media in no time. Don't worry, we've done this before. The world will be talking about what we want it to talk about in the next few minutes."

The camera flipped around to show Tommy's face. "I hope so, because if this doesn't work, we're toast."

Maliit na Bahay, Mindanao, The Philippines

Tommy's heart hammered as the roar of truck engines on the road below could no longer be ignored. The convoy reported only minutes ago was arriving, along with whoever was inside.

They were about to be overwhelmed by possibly hundreds of soldiers here for the gold, and to silence any who knew about it.

"Here comes that helicopter," said Leather, shielding his eyes to the east. "If you're going to do something, you better bloody well do it now."

Tommy ignored the pressure, instead focusing on the job at hand. He held the camera out, steadying Bautista in the frame. "Are you ready, Professor?"

A clearly camera-shy Bautista nodded, sweat on his forehead, his entire body tense.

"Okay, sir, you're live."

Bautista stood there, saying nothing.

"You're live, Professor, you can start speaking now."

313

Bautista's eyes were wide, his face pale as the soldiers coming up the hill were impossible to ignore, the thumping of rotors threatening to overwhelm the microphone. "Umm, what do I say?"

"Tell them who you are and where you are. Why we're here."

"Of course." He waved at the camera. "Umm, hello Internet. I'm Professor Buwan Bautista. I'm an archaeology professor at the University of the Philippines in Manila. I'm currently standing at a site in Mindanao, an island in the Philippines. Behind me is the entrance to a cave where we found what we believe to be tens of billions of dollars in gold, stolen by the Japanese during World War Two. Some of you may have heard of it before. It's been called Yamashita's Gold or Yamashita's Treasure."

Bautista took a step back and Tommy glanced over his shoulder to see dozens of armed troops rushing into the clearing, spreading out in a line, their weapons aimed at him and the others, several shouting orders.

"Th-they want us to surrender!" hissed Bautista, his hands slowly rising.

Tommy turned and took footage of the soldiers then flipped the camera onto himself. "My name is Tommy Granger. I'm a grad student at St. Paul's University in Maryland. I'm here with my professor, James Acton, and his wife Professor Laura Palmer from the Smithsonian, and my girlfriend Mai Trinh, also a grad student." He made sure to get a shot of them. "We are unarmed and innocent. We need everyone watching this to spread the word. We need you to protect us from what's about to happen. These people want to steal the gold and hide the truth. There are hundreds of bodies inside that cave. An entire village was slaughtered

314

by the Japanese years ago to protect this secret. You should be able to see the footage on your screens now.

"Earlier today, we were kidnapped by soldiers pretending to be terrorists, then they tried to kill us. Luckily, we were rescued, but now we're here, risking our lives to protect this treasure from being looted once again. This doesn't belong to these people, it belongs to the victims. It belongs to those it was stolen from, and it belongs to the Filipino people who suffered during the occupation. We need you to save us. Share the link, let everyone know, and start calling your politicians, let them know what is going on. Spread the word and save not only our lives, but the legacy of this village that was destroyed. Our lives are in your hands."

Operations Center 2, CIA Headquarters

Langley, Virginia

"The kid's good."

Leroux agreed with Morrison's assessment. "The kid has a hit podcast. He's actually pretty popular."

"Holy shit!" cried Child as he spun in his chair. "Check out those numbers!"

Leroux glanced at the counter showing how many were watching the broadcast and smiled. They had just rolled one million, and with each update, another hundred-thousand were added, the build rapid. "Please tell me the Filipinos are seeing this."

Morrison nodded. "My understanding is the president himself is watching it."

"Then this is going to work?"

Morrison frowned. "Only if one of those soldiers, who has probably been promised millions of dollars to keep their mouths shut, is willing to obey an order from their commander in chief."

Maliit na Bahay, Mindanao, The Philippines

The chopper landed and Ocampo threw open the door. The Americanos were at the cave entrance, one of them pointing a cellphone at him. He laughed.

What good will that do you? We're nowhere near a cellphone tower.

The pilot powered down, the thunder of the Huey's rotors quickly fading, and Ocampo turned to his men, sweeping his arm forward. "Arrest these people!"

The young man with the cellphone stepped forward. "Sir, you're live with the world. I'd be very careful what you do."

Ocampo's eyes narrowed. "What are you talking about?"

"This phone is attached to a satellite uplink. The video I'm taking right now is being broadcast to the entire world over the Internet. We currently have over"—he paused, as if listening to someone—"five million people watching this right now."

Ocampo shook his head, a leer spreading. "I don't care. Once I have what's inside that cave, I'm untouchable. So are all these men. I can kill you now, take the gold, and before anyone can get here to help you, I'll be long gone, and we'll all be rich." He drew his weapon and advanced with his men. "You've lost, my boy."

"Let me take him out, BD."

Dawson watched the proceedings through the scope of his weapon, as eager as Niner was to eliminate the new arrival. "Just wait. Everybody got their targets?"

A string of ayes.

"Hold for my command."

He adjusted his scope. Colonel Ocampo was his. It was him and his cousin that had been the cause of all this, who had put his men in harm's way, who had kidnapped then tried to kill his friends.

He would be the first to go down.

But only if it were necessary.

He had the Sea Hawk drop them only a few miles away, then they had hoofed back, sending the chopper on its way in case they were monitored. He wanted the Filipinos to think the civilians were on their own, without protection, so they would have the element of surprise should it become necessary.

"Something's happening," said Atlas. "Check the chopper."

Acton burst with pride over Tommy's speech. It was heartfelt and so adultlike, his esteem for the boy—scratch that, man—was swelling. Yet he feared none of it would make any difference now, though the epitaph it left for them all was honorable.

Laura squeezed his hand and he looked at her, her eyes darting toward the helicopter, its rotors now idle. He turned his head to see the pilot rounding the front of the aircraft, drawing his weapon. Acton instinctively put himself in front of Laura and Mai, then his jaw dropped when the pilot pressed the weapon against the new arrival's back.

"Colonel, you are under arrest by order of the President," said the pilot in English, likely for the benefit of the viewing audience at home. He shouted something in Filipino, repeating it several times, and finally a few in the line of soldiers broke formation, stepping backward then turning to flee down the hill and to their trucks below.

The rest followed suit.

Acton whispered to Bautista. "What did he say?"

"He said that the President was willing to forgive their actions if they left immediately, but would have them executed if they remained."

Leather walked over to the pilot and handed him a zip tie, the man quickly binding his prisoner's hands then putting him back in the chopper. His prisoner secure, he holstered his weapon and returned to join the group, facing Tommy's camera.

"On behalf of the President of the Philippines, I would like to apologize for everything that has happened to you. He would also like to say that he appreciates your efforts in locating the missing gold, and assures you that Professor Bautista will be in charge of its cataloging."

Bautista exchanged an excited grin with the group, then walked forward, extending a trembling hand. "You have our thanks, sir, for saving us."

The pilot shook Bautista's hand then bowed his head. "I was just doing my job, sir. Now, if you'll excuse me, I have to report back to command what has happened."

Tommy pointed at the camera. "I think they already know."

"Well, I think we can safely leave now."

Niner agreed with Dawson. "Let's. Have you seen some of the bugs here? It's freakin' insane!"

Atlas eyed him. "You're from Korea. Aren't you used to them?"

"I'm from America, and just because my eyes are different than yours, doesn't mean I come from a jungle. Take a look at a map. South Korea hosted the damned Winter Olympics."

Atlas thrust his lips out, staring down at Niner. "So, what you're saying is you're a coward."

Niner pointed at Atlas' shoulder. "There's a three-foot centipede on your back."

Atlas twisted his head as he reached for his back, spinning like a dog chasing his tail. "Get it off! Get it off!"

Niner roared with laughter along with the others as their friend tried to rid himself of an imaginary insect. "Yeah, *I'm* the coward."

The Lotus

Tokyo, Japan

Takashi lay on the couch, his head in the lap of his "nurse," drifting in and out of consciousness as she gently stroked his hair, her pleas for Akira to let him go long stopped.

Akira was content to let him die.

He wasn't certain why, though he suspected it was an act of defiance in the face of his father. If Akira laid his hands on the gold first, then he might attempt to usurp his father with a promise of riches to the other Yakuza leadership.

Yet at this moment, he didn't care about their politics, or his own life for that matter.

He just wanted to die, the pain too much.

And he was certain he'd get his wish any moment.

Shouts in the distance went ignored in his fog. Men shouted, women screamed, and the blurred view he had of the world became confused as new arrivals rushed about.

"Please, help him! I think he's dying!"

It was his nurse, renewing her pleas, but this time someone heeded them, and he felt hands on him, moments later lifting him onto something. He was being pushed now, every sensation changing.

Except the hand that still gripped his, and the concerned voice of his angel protector.

And as he felt the cool night air on his skin, and registered the flashing of lights surrounding him, he finally realized he had been saved.

And the Kijima family's ordeal was finally over.

City Garden Grand Hotel
Manila, The Philippines

Acton put the phone down then leaned back in his chair, the sitting area of their hotel occupied by Laura, Tommy, Mai, and Leather. Bautista was at the site, having the time of his life, he was certain, and they hadn't seen Bravo Team since they had left them.

Though he had a feeling they had never really gone that far.

"Dylan says he'll pass our thanks on to the guys."

Laura took his hand. "I really wish there was something we could do for them. Like set up scholarships for all their kids or something."

"Wouldn't that be bribery?" asked Tommy.

Acton chuckled. "I don't know. Might be. I'm sure there's some charity though that we could donate to. Help them out indirectly."

Laura smiled. "Let's look into it when we're home."

Tommy cleared his throat. "So, will there be some sort of finder's fee or something?"

Laura shook her head, a wide smile on her face. "Nooo, and if there were, it would be going to Buwan, not us."

Mai swatted his arm. "Don't be greedy."

"Speaking of greed," said Tommy, "when will we be home? My podcast subscribers have quadrupled since our little escapade. I think I'm going to be able to start making some real coin from advertising."

Acton laughed. "Tommy, our Internet star." He leaned forward. "I'm sure you haven't missed out on the irony of what just happened."

Tommy's eyes narrowed, the young man evidently having indeed missed it. "What do you mean?"

"Well, if your blockchain thing had been in place, the CIA would never have been able to use all their fake accounts to drive traffic to the live feed, and we'd all be dead."

Tommy's eyes bulged. "Holy shit! I never thought of that!"

Acton's phone vibrated with a message. He swiped his thumb. "It's from Hugh. He says that Takashi kid the Yakuza were holding is going to be all right, and apparently his great-grandfather is already being questioned about his involvement in the massacre."

Leather leaped to his feet. "Bloody hell!"

Acton tensed. "What?"

"I forgot I tied up two Yakuza and left them! They're still there!"

Parang, The Philippines
September 3rd, 2006

Juan sat propped up in his bed, his body a shadow of its former self. He was dying. He knew it, it was obvious, though those that surrounded him were in denial. He was fine with it. After all, he should be dead. He alone had survived, and his adopted mother, Marikit, had been right. He had forgotten. All he had left were his words, written down all those years ago, capturing the memories that would eventually fade, and preserving them for time immemorial.

Yet he couldn't bring himself to read them.

They simply brought too much pain.

One of his grandsons rushed into the room. "Grandpa, the man from the university is here!"

Juan smiled weakly, shuffling into a more upright position before making certain he was decent enough to receive such a distinguished guest. In the over sixty years since his village had been wiped out, he had never heard mention of it, and was determined that it shouldn't be forgotten to history. He had sent a letter—for his new mother and father had kept their promise and he had learned to read and write—to the government, asking for their help in preserving his writings, and he had heard back many months later.

They were sending someone.

A man walked into the room, a broad smile on his face, his hand extended. "Juan, I'm so pleased to finally meet you. My name is Professor Buwan Bautista. I understand you have something you'd like to share with our countrymen."

The moment became all too real. Until this moment, until right now, he alone remembered the village he had once called home, the parents that had once loved him, the villagers that he had called his friends. But now he was about to fulfill his promise made so long ago. Today he would preserve their memory for all eternity.

Tears rolled down his cheeks as he pointed to the stack of papers sitting nearby.

"Those tell the story of my people. Everything I could remember at the time. They are the memories of a little boy, who knew nothing of the world, yet only knew that those poor innocents were his entire world, and everyone he had ever loved."

Bautista nodded gravely, then sat at the table and began to read, his own tears flowing. He held up one of the pages and Juan immediately recognized it as the first he had written.

"Did you ever find it? Someone to love you?"

Juan smiled and held out his hand, his wife of over fifty years joining him, sitting on the edge of the bed, his sons and daughters gathered in the doorway, his grandchildren at their feet.

All the love a man could ever want in a lifetime.

"Yes, I did."

THE END

ACKNOWLEDGMENTS

When I was researching this book, I had a pretty good idea of what I wanted, and began a loose plot. As the research continued, we stumbled upon a story about the treasure having already been found.

This sort of threw a monkey wrench into things.

As I continued to read, I realized it wasn't really a problem, and the Roxas discovery mentioned in the novel was easily addressed as a decoy, and was usefully employed as a means of casting doubt on Takashi's great-grandfather's claims.

Nearing the release date of this novel, I received an email from a reader who had just received the newsletter notification about the subject matter of the upcoming book, and he informed me he was involved in the court case mentioned earlier.

It's a small world!

On a more serious note, in this novel, there is a reference to "comfort women." This was the term used by the Japanese during World War Two for the hundreds of thousands of women taken prisoner by the Japanese Imperial Army and used as sex slaves for their soldiers around the region. The ordeal these women went through is unthinkable, and shows how history repeats itself when recent events involving ISIS are brought into the discussion.

As usual, there are people to thank. My dad for all the research, Susan "Miss Boss" Turnbull for a grammar save, Brent Richards for some weapons and hand-to-hand combat info, and, as always, my wife, daughter, and mother, as well as the proofing team.

To those who have not already done so, please visit my website at www.jrobertkennedy.com then sign up for the Insider's Club to be notified of new book releases. Your email address will never be shared or sold, and you'll only receive the occasional email from me, as I don't have time to spam you!

Thank you once again for reading.